FANTASTIC VOYAGE

A NOVEL BY ISAAC ASIMOV

BASED ON THE SCREENPLAY BY

HARRY KLEINER FROM THE ORIGINAL

STORY BY OTTO KLEMENT AND

JAY LEWIS BIXBY

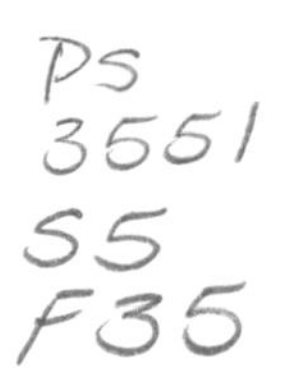

HOUGHTON MIFFLIN COMPANY BOSTON

w 15 14 13

Library of Congress Catalog Card
Number: 66-12593
ISBN: 0-395-07352-9

Printed in the United States of America

DEDICATION

TO MARC AND MARCIA

WHO TWISTED MY ARM

PREFACE

THIS STORY, which has grown into both a book and a film, has several authors, all of whom have contributed to its present form in many different ways. For all of us, it was a long and arduous task and a great challenge, but also one of deep satisfaction and, I may say, of great delight. When Jay L. Bixby and I wrote our original story, little did we know where it would lead or what would become of it in the hands of men of great imagination and superb artistry — Saul David, the film's producer; Richard Fleischer, the director and inspired conjurer of fancy; Harry Kleiner, who wrote the screenplay; Dale Hennesy, the art director and an artist in his own right; and the doctors and scientists who gave us so much of their time and their thinking. And finally, Isaac Asimov, who lent his pen and great talent to give form and reality to this phantasmagoria of facts and fancy.

OTTO KLEMENT

CONTENTS

1 PLANE, *1*

2 CAR, *15*

3 HEADQUARTERS, *23*

4 BRIEFING, *35*

5 SUBMARINE, *53*

6 MINIATURIZATION, *69*

7 SUBMERGENCE, *79*

8 ENTRY, *89*

9 ARTERY, *101*

10 HEART, *115*

11 CAPILLARY, *129*

12 LUNG, *141*

13 PLEURA, *157*

14 LYMPHATIC, *171*

15 EAR, *183*

16 BRAIN, *201*

17 CLOT, *211*

18 EYE, *225*

FANTASTIC VOYAGE

CHAPTER 1 PLANE

It was an old plane, a four-engine plasma jet that had been retired from active service, and it came in along a route that was neither economical nor particularly safe. It nosed through the cloud banks on a trip that took it twelve hours where five might have sufficed with a rocket-powered supersonic.

And there was well over an hour to go.

The agent aboard knew that his part of the job wouldn't be finished till the plane touched down and that the last hour would be the longest.

He glanced at the only other man in the large passenger cabin — napping for the moment, with his chin buried in his chest.

The passenger didn't look particularly striking or impressive but at the moment he was the most important man in the world.

*

General Alan Carter looked up glumly when the colonel walked in. Carter's eyes were pouchy and the corners of his mouth sagged. He tried to bend the paper clip he was manhandling back into shape and it flicked out of his hand.

"Nearly got me that time," said Colonel Donald Reid, calmly. His sandy hair lay back smoothly but his short, graying mustache bristled. He wore his uniform with the same indefinable unnaturalness that the other did. Both were specialists, drafted for work in a super-specialty, with military rank for convenience and, considering the applications of the field, somewhat out of necessity.

Both had the CMDF insignia. Each letter was in a small hexagon, two above, three below. The middle hexagon of the three bore a symbol that further classified the man. In the case of Reid, it was a caduceus, marking him as a medical man.

"Guess what I'm doing," said the general.

"Flipping paper clips."

"Sure. And counting the hours, too. Like a fool!" His voice rose a controlled notch. "I sit here with my hands wet, my hair sticky, my heart pounding, and I count the hours. Only now it's the minutes. Seventy-two minutes, Don. Seventy-two minutes and they're down at the airport."

"All right. Why be nervous, then? Is there anything wrong?"

"No. Nothing. He was picked up safely. He was taken right out of Their hands with, as far as we know, not a hitch. He got safely into the plane, an old one . . ."

"Yes. I know."

Carter shook his head. He wasn't interested in telling the other something new; he was interested in talking. "We figured that They would figure that We would figure time was of the utmost importance, so that We would pile him into an X-52 and rocket him through inner space. Only We figured They would figure that and have the anti-missile network at saturation level . . ."

Reid said, "Paranoia, we call it in my profession. I mean,

for anyone to believe They'd do that. They'd risk war and annihilation."

"They might risk just that to stop what's happening. I'd almost feel We ought to risk it if the situation were reversed. So We took a commercial plane, a four-engine plasma jet. I was wondering if it could take off, it was so old."

"Did it?"

"Did it what?" For a moment, the general had sunk into blackened thought.

"Take off?"

"Yes, yes. It's coming along fine. I get my reports from Grant."

"Who's he?"

"The agent in charge. I know him. With him in charge, I feel as safe as it is possible to feel, which isn't much. Grant ran the whole thing; flicked Benes out of Their hands like a seed out of a watermelon."

"Well, then?"

"But I still worry. I tell you, Reid, there's only one safe way of handling matters in this damned racket. You've got to believe They're as smart as We are; that for every trick We've got, They've got a counter-trick; that for every man We've got planted on Their side, They've got one planted on Ours. This has been going on for over half a century now; we've *got* to be evenly matched, or it would have been all over long ago."

"Take it easy, Al."

"How can I? This thing *now*, this thing Benes is bringing with him, this new knowledge, may end the stalemate once and for all. And with Ourselves as winners."

Reid said, "I hope the Others don't think so, too. If they do . . . you know, Al, so far there have been rules to this game. One side doesn't do anything to back the other side into a corner so tight he has to use his missile buttons. You've got to leave him a safe ledge to step back on. Push hard but not too hard. When Benes gets here, They may get the notion They're being pushed too hard."

"We have no choice but to risk that." Then, as the afterthought plagued him, "*If* he gets here."

"He will, won't he?"

Carter had risen to his feet, as though to begin a hasty walk back and forth to nowhere. He stared at the other, then sat down abruptly. "All right, why get excited? You've got that tranquilizer gleam in your eye, Doctor. I don't need any happy pills. But suppose he does get here in seventy-two — sixty-six minutes. Suppose he lands at the airport. He's still got to be brought here, to be kept here, safely. There's many a slip . . ."

"Twixt the cup and the lip," singsonged Reid. "For God's sake, General, shall we be sensible and talk about consequences? I mean — what happens after he gets here?"

"Come on, Don, let's wait for that till he does get here."

"Come on, Al," mimicked the colonel, an edge appearing on his own words. "It won't do to wait till he gets here. It will be too late when he gets here. You'll be too busy, then, and all the little ants at the Pentagon will start rushing about madly, so that nothing will get done where I think it needs to be done."

"I promise . . ." The general's gesture was a vague one of dismissal.

Reid ignored it. "No. You're going to be unable to keep any promise you make for the future. Call the chief now, will you? *Now!* You can get through to him. Right now, you're the only one who can get through to him. Get him to understand that CMDF isn't the handmaiden of defense only. Or if you can't, get in touch with Commissioner Furnald. He's on our side. Tell him I want some crumbs for the bio-sciences. Point out there are votes on this. Look, Al, we've got to have a voice loud enough to be heard. We've got to have some fighting chance. Once Benes gets here and is jumped by all the real generals, damn them, we'll be out of commission forever."

"I can't, Don. And I won't. If you want it straight, I'm not doing a damned thing till I've got Benes here. And I don't take it kindly your trying to put the arm on me at this time."

Reid's lips went white. "What am I supposed to do, General?"

"Wait as I am waiting. Count the minutes."

Reid turned to go. His anger remained under tight control. "I'd reconsider the tranquilizer if I were you, general."

Carter watched him go without comment. He looked at his watch. "Sixty-one minutes!" he muttered, and groped for a paper clip.

*

It was almost with relief that Reid stepped into the office of Dr. Michaels, the civilian head of the Medical Division. The expression on Michaels' broad face might never move higher than a quiet cheerfulness accompanied by, at most, a dry chuckle, but, on the other hand, it never dropped lower than a twinkling solemnity that never took itself, it would seem, too seriously.

He had the inevitable chart in his hand, or one of them. To Colonel Reid, all those charts were alike, all a hopeless maze, and taken together, they were hopelessness many times compounded.

Occasionally, Michaels would try to explain the charts to him, or to almost anyone — Michaels was pathetically eager to explain it all.

The blood stream, it seemed, was tagged with a trace of mild radioactivity and the organism (it could be a man or a mouse) then took its own photograph, so to speak, on a laserized principle that produced a three-dimensional image.

"Well, never mind that," Michaels would say at that point. "You get a picture of the entire circulatory system in three dimensions which can then be recorded two-dimensionally in as large a number of sections and projections as would be required for the job. You could get down to the smallest capillaries, if the picture were properly enlarged.

"And that leaves me just a geographer," Michaels would add. "A geographer of the human body, plotting its rivers and bays, its inlets and streams; much more complicated than anything on Earth, I assure you."

Reid looked at the chart over Michaels' shoulder and said, "Whose is that, Max?"

"No one's to speak of." Michaels tossed it aside. "I'm waiting, that's all. When someone else waits, he reads a book. I read a blood system."

"You're waiting, too, eh? So's he." Reid's head nodded backward in the direction of Carter's office. "Waiting for the same thing?"

"For Benes to get here. Of course. And yet, you know, I don't entirely believe it."

"Don't believe what?"

"I'm not sure the man has what he says he has. I'm a physiologist, to be sure, and not a physicist," Michaels shrugged in self-deprecatory humor, "but I like to believe the experts. They say there's no way. I hear them say that the Uncertainty Principle makes it impossible to do it for longer than a given time. And you can't argue with the Uncertainty Principle, can you?"

"I'm no expert either, Max, but those same experts tell us that Benes is the biggest expert of them all in this field. The Other Side has had him and They've kept even with Us just because of him; *just* because of him. They have no one else in the first rank, while We have Zaletsky, Kramer, Richtheim, Lindsay, and all the rest. And our biggest men believe he must have something, if he says he does."

"Do They? Or do They just think we can't afford not to take

a chance on it? After all, even if he turns c
We win just out of his defection. The Oth
have the use of his service."

"Why should he lie?"

Michaels said, "Why not? It's gettir
him here, where I suppose he wants to be. If
nothing, we're not going to send him back, are we?
may not be lying; he may just be mistaken."

"Hmph," Reid tilted his chair back and put his feet on the desk in most un-colonel-like manner. "You've got a point there. And if he diddles us, it would serve Carter right. Serve them all right. Damned fools."

"You got nothing out of Carter, eh?"

"Nothing. He won't do a thing till Benes comes. He's counting the minutes and now so am I. It's forty-two minutes."

"Till when?"

"Till the plane carrying him lands at the airport. And the bio-sciences have nothing. If Benes is just pulling off a deal to escape from the Other Side, we have nothing; and if it's legitimate, we'll still have nothing. Defense will take it all, every slice, every crumb, every smell. It will be too pretty to play with and they'll never let it go."

"Nonsense. Maybe just at first they will hang on, but we have our pressures, too. We can turn Duval loose on them; the intense, God-fearing Peter."

A look of distaste came across Reid's face. "I would love to throw him at the military. The way I feel now, I would love to throw him at Carter, too. If Duval were negatively charged and Carter positively charged and I could get them together and let them spark each other to death . . ."

"Don't get destructive, Don. You take Duval too seriously. A surgeon is an artist, a sculptor of living tissue. A great surgeon is a great artist and has the temperament of one."

ell, *I* have temperament, too, and I don't use it to be one
e pain in the buttocks. What gives Duval a monopoly on
e right to be an offensive, arrogant son of a bitch?"

"If he had the monopoly, my Colonel, I would be delighted. I would leave it to him with all possible gratitude, if he had it all. The trouble is there are so many other offensive, arrogant sons of bitches in the world."

"I suppose so. I suppose so," muttered Reid, but he was unmollified. "Thirty-seven minutes."

*

If anyone had repeated Reid's capsule description of Duval to Dr. Peter Lawrence Duval, it would have been met with the same short grunt that would have met a confession of love. It was not that Duval was insensible to either insult or adoration, it was merely that he reacted to them when he had time, and he rarely had time. It was not a scowl that he habitually wore on his face, it was rather the muscular contraction that came with thoughts that were elsewhere. Presumably all men have their escape from the world; Duval's was the simple one of concentration upon his work. That route had brought him by his mid-forties to international renown as a brain surgeon, and to his scarce-realized status of bachelorhood.

Nor did he look up from the careful measurements he was making on the tri-dimensionalized X-ray photographs that lay before him when the door opened. His assistant came in with the accustomed noiseless steps.

"What is it, Miss Peterson?" he asked, and squinted even more painfully at the photographs. The depth-perception was plain enough to the eye, but measuring the actual depth called for a delicate consideration of angles, plus an advance knowledge of what that depth was likely to be in the first place.

Cora Peterson waited for the moment of additional concentration to pass. She was twenty-five, just twenty years younger than Duval, and her master's degree, only a year old, had been carefully laid at the feet of the surgeon.

In the letters she wrote home, she explained almost every time that each day with Duval was a college course; that to study his methods, his techniques of diagnosis, his handling of the tools of his trade was to be edified beyond belief. As for his dedication to his work and to the cause of healing, that could only be described as inspiring.

In less intellectualized fashion, she was perfectly aware, with almost the awareness of a professional physiologist, of the quickening of her heartbeat as she took in the planes and curves of his face bent over his work and noted the quick, sure, unwavering motion of his fingers. Her face remained impassive, however, for she disapproved of the action of her unintellectual heart muscle.

Her mirror told her, clearly enough, that she was not plain. Quite otherwise. Her dark eyes were ingenuously wide-set; her lips reflected quick humor when she let them do so — which wasn't often; and her figure annoyed her for its apparent propensity for interfering with the proper understanding of her professional competence. It was for her ability she wanted wolf-whistles (or the intellectual equivalent) and not for the sinuosity she couldn't help.

Duval, at least, appreciated her efficiency and seemed unmoved by her attractiveness and for that she admired him the more.

She said, finally, "Benes will be landing in less than thirty minutes, Doctor."

"Hmm." He looked up. "Why are you here? Your day's over."

Cora might have retorted that his was, too, but she knew well that his day was over only when his work was done. She had stayed with him through the sixteenth consecutive hour often enough, although she imagined he would maintain (in all honesty) that he kept her firmly to an eight-hour day.

She said, "I'm waiting to see him."

"Whom?"

"Benes. Doesn't it excite you, Doctor?"

"No. Why should it?"

"He's a great scientist, and they say he has important information that will revolutionize all we're doing."

"It will, will it?" Duval lifted the photograph on top of the heap, placed it to one side, and turned to the next. "How will it help you with your laser work?"

"It can make the target easier to hit."

"It already does that. For what Benes will add, only the war makers will have any use. All Benes will do will be to increase the probability of world destruction."

"But Dr. Duval, you've said that the extension of the technique could be of great importance to the neurophysiologist."

"Have I? All right, then, I have. But just the same I'd rather you got your proper rest, Miss Peterson." He looked up again (his voice softening just a bit, perhaps?), "You look tired."

Cora's hand lifted halfway to her hair, for translated into the feminine, the word "tired" means "disheveled." She said, "Once Benes arrives, I will. I promise. By the way . . ."

"Yes?"

"Will you be using the laser tomorrow?"

"It's what I'm trying to decide right now—if you'll let me, Miss Peterson."

"The 6951 model can't be used."

Duval put the photograph down, leaned back. "Why not?"

"It's not reliable enough. I can't get it to focus properly. I suspect one of the tunnel diodes is faulty but I haven't located which one yet."

"All right. You set up one that can be trusted just in case we need it and do it before you leave. Then, tomorrow . . ."

"Then tomorrow I'll track down what's wrong with the 6951."

"Yes."

She turned to leave, looked quickly at her watch, and said, "Twenty-one minutes — and they say the plane's on time."

He made a vague sound and she knew he hadn't heard. She left, closing the door behind her slowly and silently.

*

Captain William Owens sank back into the softly cushioned seat of the limousine. He rubbed his sharp nose tiredly and set his wide jaws. He felt the car lift on its firm jets of compressed air, then move forward with absolute levelness. He caught no whisper of the turbo-engine, though five hundred horses champed behind him.

Through the bulletproof windows to right and left he could see a motorcycle escort. Other cars were before and behind, glimmering the night into a liveness of shielded light.

It made him seem important, this half an army of guardians, but it wasn't for him, of course. It wasn't even for the man they were going out to meet; not for the man as a man. Only for the contents of a great mind.

The head of the Secret Service was to Owens' left. It was a sign of the anonymity of the Service that Owens was not sure of the name of this nondescript man who, from rimless glasses to conservative shoes, seemed a college professor — or a haberdasher's clerk.

"Colonel Gander," Owens had said, tentatively, on shaking hands.

"Gonder," was the quiet response. "Good evening, Captain Owens."

They were on the outskirts of the airfield, now. Somewhere above and ahead, surely not more than a few miles distant, was the archaic plane, preparing for a landing.

"A great day, eh?" said Gonder, softly. Everything about the man seemed to whisper, even the unobtrusive cut of his civilian clothing.

"Yes," said Owens, striving to keep the tension out of that monosyllable. It was not that he felt particularly tense, it was merely that his voice always seemed to carry that tone. It was that air of tension that seemed to fit his narrow, pinched nose, his slitted eyes, and the high jut of his cheekbones.

He sometimes felt it got in his way. People expected him to be neurotic when he wasn't. Not more so than others were, anyway. On the other hand, people sometimes got out of his way for just that reason, without his having to lift a hand. Matters evened out, perhaps.

Owens said, "Quite a coup, getting him here. The Service is to be congratulated."

"The credit belongs to our agent. He's our best man. His secret, I think, is that he looks like the romantic stereotype of an agent."

"Looks like one?"

"Tall. Played football at college. Good-looking. Terribly clean-cut. One look at him and any enemy would say: There. That's what one of Their secret agents ought to look like, so of course, he can't be one. And they dismiss him and find out too late that he *is* one."

Owens frowned. Was the man serious? Or was he joking because he thought that would relieve the tension?

Gonder said, "You realize, of course, that your part in this isn't something to be dismissed offhand. You will know him, won't you?"

"I'll know him," said Owens, with his short, nervous laugh. "I've met him several times at scientific conferences on the

Other Side. I got drunk with him one night; well, not really drunk—joyous."

"Did he talk?"

"I didn't get him drunk to make him talk. But anyway, he didn't talk. There was someone else with him. Their scientists go two by two at all times."

"Did *you* talk?" The question was light; the intent behind it was clearly not.

Owens laughed again. "Believe me, Colonel, there is nothing I know that he doesn't. I could talk to him all day without harm."

"I wish I knew something about this. You have my admiration, Captain. Here is a technological miracle capable of transforming the world and there are only a handful of men who can understand it. Man's mind is getting away from man."

"It's not that bad, really," said Owens. "There are quite a lot of us. There's only one Benes, of course, and I'm miles from being in *his* class. In fact, I don't know much more than enough to apply the technique to my ship designs. That's all."

"But you'll recognize Benes?" The Secret Service head seemed to require infinite reassurance.

"Even if he had a twin brother, which I'm sure he doesn't, I'd recognize him."

"It's not exactly an academic point, Captain. Our agent, Grant, is good, as I've said, but even so I am a little surprised that he managed it. I have to ask myself: is there a double double cross involved? Did They expect Us to try to get Benes and have They prepared a pseudo-Benes?"

"I can tell the difference," said Owens, confidently.

"You don't know what can be done these days with plastic surgery and narco-hypnosis."

"It doesn't matter. The face can fool me, but the conversation won't. Either he knows the Technique" (Owen's momentary whisper clearly capitalized the word) "better than I do or he's not Benes, whatever he looks like. They can fake Benes' body, perhaps, but not his mind."

They were on the field now. Colonel Gonder looked at his watch. "I hear it. The ship will be landing in minutes — and on time."

Armed men and armored vehicles splayed out to join those that had already surrounded the airfield and turned it into occupied territory sealed off against all but authorized personnel.

The last of the city's lights had faded out, doing no more than to fuzz the horizon to the left.

Owens' sigh was one of infinite relief. Benes would be here, at last, in one more moment.

Happy ending?

He frowned at the intonation in his mind that had put a question mark after those two words.

Happy ending! he thought grimly, but the intonation slithered out of control so that it became Happy ending? again.

CHAPTER 2 CAR

GRANT WATCHED with intense relief the lights of the city drawing nearer as the plane began its long approach. No one had given him any real details as to the importance of Dr. Benes — except for the obvious fact that he was a defecting scientist with vital information. He was the most important man in the world, they had said — and then had neglected to explain why.

Don't press, they had told him. Don't throw the grease in the fan by getting tense. But the whole thing is vital, they said. Unbelievably vital.

Take it easy, they had said, but everything depends on it; your country, your world, humanity.

So it was done. He might never have made it if They hadn't been afraid of killing Benes. By the time They got to the point where They realized that killing Benes was the only way They could salvage even a draw, it was too late and he was out. A bullet crease over the ribs was all Grant had to show for it, and a long Band-Aid took care of that.

He was tired now, however, tired to the bone. Physically tired, of course, but also tired of the whole damned foolishness. In his college days, ten years before, they had called him Granite Grant and he had tried to live up to that on the football field, like a dumb jerk. One broken arm was the result but at least he was lucky enough to have kept his teeth and nose intact so that he could retain that craggy set of good looks. (His lips twitched into a silent, flicking smile.)

And since then, too, he had discouraged the use of first names. Only the monosyllabic grunt of Grant. Very masculine. Very strong.

Except to hell with it. What was it getting him except weariness and every prospect of a short life? He had just passed thirty now and it was time to retire to his first name. Charles Grant. Maybe even Charlie Grant. Good Old Charlie Grant!

He winced, but then frowned himself firm again. It *had* to be. Good Old Charlie. That was it. Good old soft Charlie who likes to sit in a rocking chair and rock. Hi, Charlie, nice day. Hey there, Charlie, looks like rain. Get yourself a soft job, good old Charlie, and snooze your way to your pension.

Grant looked sideways at Jan Benes. Even he found something familiar about that shock of grizzled hair, the face with its strong, fleshy nose, the untidy, coarse mustache, likewise grizzled. Cartoonists made do with that nose and mustache alone, but there were his eyes, too, nestled in fine wrinkles, and there were the horizontal lines that never left his forehead.

Benes' clothes were moderately ill fitting, but they had left hurriedly, without time for the better tailors. The scientist was pushing fifty, Grant knew, but he looked older.

Benes was leaning forward, watching the lights of the approaching city.

Grant said, "Ever been to this part of the country before, Professor?"

"I have never been to any part of your country," said Benes, "or was that intended to be a trick question?" There was a faint but definite trace of accent in his speech.

"No. Just making conversation. That's our second largest city up ahead. You can have it, though. I'm from the other end of the country."

"To me it doesn't matter. One end. The other end. As long as I'm here. It will be . . ." He didn't finish the sentence but there was a sadness in his eyes.

Breaking away is hard, thought Grant, even when you feel you must. He said, "We'll see to it you have no time to brood, Professor. We'll put you to work."

Benes retained his sadness. "I'm sure of that. I expect it. It is the price I pay, no?"

"I'm afraid so. You caused us a certain amount of effort, you know."

Benes put his hand on Grant's sleeve. "You risked your life. I appreciate that. You might have been killed."

"I run the chance of being killed as a matter of routine. Occupational hazard. They pay me for it. Not as well as for playing a guitar, you understand, or for hitting a baseball, but about what they feel my life is worth."

"You can't dismiss it so."

"I've got to. My organization does. When I come back, there will be a shake of hands and an embarrassed 'Good work!' You know, manly reserve and all that. Then it's: 'Now for the next assignment and we have to deduct for that band-aid you have on your side. Have to watch expenses.'"

"Your game of cynicism doesn't fool me, young man."

"It has to fool *me*, Professor, or I would quit." Grant was almost surprised at the sudden bitterness in his voice. "Strap yourself in, Professor. This flying junk heap makes rough landings."

•

The plane touched down smoothly, despite Grant's prediction, and taxied to a stop, turning as it did so.

The Secret Service contingent closed in. Soldiers leaped out of troop-carrying trucks to form a cordon about the plane, leaving a corridor for the motorized stairway steering its way toward the door of the plane.

A convoy of three limousines rolled to near the foot of the stairway.

Owens said, "You're piling on the security, Colonel."

"Better too much than too little." His lips moved almost silently in what the astonished Owens recognized to be a quick prayer.

Owens said, "I'm glad he's here."

"Not as glad as I am. Planes have blown up in mid-flight before this, you know. We'll get him on terra firma."

The door to the plane opened and Grant momentarily appeared at the opening. He looked about, then waved.

Colonel Gonder said, "*He* seems in one piece anyway. Where's Benes?"

As though in answer to that question, Grant flattened to one side and let Benes squeeze past. Benes stood there smiling for one moment. Carrying one battered suitcase in his hand, he trotted gingerly down the steps. Grant followed. Behind him were the pilot and copilot.

Colonel Gonder was at the foot of the stairs. "Professor Benes. Glad to have you here! I'm Gonder; I'll be in charge of your safety from this point. This is William Owens. You know him, I think."

Benes' eyes lit up and his arms went high as he dropped his suitcase. (Colonel Gonder unobtrusively picked it up.)

"Owens! Yes, of course. We got drunk one night together. I remember it well. A long, dull, boring session in the afternoon, where all that was interesting was precisely what one could *not* say, so that despair settled on me like a gray blanket. At supper, Owens and I met. There were five of his colleagues with him, but I don't remember the others very well.

"But Owens and I, we went to a little club afterward, with dancing and jazz, and we drank schnapps, and Owens was very friendly with one of the girls. You remember Jaroslavic, Owens?"

"The fellow who was with you?" ventured Owens.

"Exactly. He loved schnapps with a love that passeth understanding, but he was not allowed to drink. He had to stay sober. Strict orders."

"To watch you?"

Benes signified assent by a single, long, vertical movement of his head and a sober out-thrusting of his lower lip. "I kept offering him liquor. I said, here, Milan, a dusty throat is bad for man, and he had to keep refusing, but with his heart in his eyes. It was wicked of me."

Owens smiled and nodded. "But let's get into the limousine and get down to headquarters. We'll have to show you around, first, and let everyone see you're here. After that, I promise you that you'll sleep for twenty-four hours if you want to before we ask you any questions."

"Sixteen will do. But first—" He looked about anxiously. "Where is Grant? Ach, *there* is Grant."

He pushed toward the young agent. "Grant!" He held out his hand. "Good-bye. Thank you. Thank you very much. I will see you again, not so?"

"Could be," said Grant. "I'm an easy man to see. Just look for the nearest rotten job, and I'll be right there on top of it."

"I'm glad you took *this* rotten one."

Grant reddened. "This rotten one had an important point to it, Professor. Glad to be of help. I mean that."

"I know. Good-bye! Good-bye!" Benes waved, stepped back toward the limousine.

Grant turned to the colonel. "Will I be breaking security if I knock off now, chief?"

"Go ahead. And by the way, Grant . . ."

"Yes, sir?"

"Good work!"

"The expression, sir, is: 'Jolly good show.' I don't answer to anything else." He touched a sardonic forefinger to his temple and walked off.

Exit, Grant, he thought, then: Enter, Good Old Charlie?

The colonel turned to Owens. "Get in with Benes and talk to him. I'll be in the car ahead. And then when we get to headquarters, I want you to be ready with a firm identification, if you have one; or a firm denial, if you have one. I don't want anything else."

"He remembered that drinking episode," said Owens.

"Exactly," said the colonel, discontentedly, "he remembered it a little too quickly and a little too well. *Talk* to him."

They were all in, and the cavalcade moved off, picking up speed. From a distance, Grant watched, waved blindly at no one in particular, then moved off again.

He had free time coming and he knew exactly how he planned spending it, after one night's sleep. He smiled in cheerful anticipation.

*

The cavalcade picked its route carefully. The pattern of bustle and calm in the city varied from section to section and from hour to hour, and that which pertained to this section and this hour was known.

The cars rumbled down empty streets through run-down neighborhoods of darkened warehouses. The motorcycles jounced on in front and the colonel in the first limousine tried once again to estimate how the Others would react to the successful coup.

Sabotage at headquarters was always a possibility. He couldn't imagine what precautions remained to be taken but it was an axiom in his business that no precautions were ever sufficient.

A light?

For just a moment, it had seemed to him that a light had flashed and dimmed in one of the hulks they were approaching. His hand flew to the telephone to alert the motorcycle escort.

He spoke quickly and fiercely. From behind, a motorcycle raced forward.

Even as it did so, an automobile engine, ahead and to one side, roared into life (muffled and nearly drowned by the multiple clatter of the oncoming cavalcade) and the automobile itself came hurtling out of an alley.

Its headlights were off and in the shock of its sudden approach, nothing registered with anyone. No one, afterward, could recall a clear picture of events.

The car-projectile, aimed squarely at the limousine containing Benes, met the motorcycle coming forward. In the crash that ensued, the motorcycle was demolished, its rider hurled many feet to one side and left broken and dead. The car-projectile itself was deflected so that it merely struck the rear of the limousine.

There were multiple collisions. The limousine, spinning out of control, smashed into a telephone pole and jolted to a stop. The kamikaze car, also out of control, hit a brick wall and burst into flame.

The colonel's limousine ground to a halt. The motorcycles screeched, veering and turning.

Gonder was out of his limousine, racing for the wrecked car, wrenching at the door.

Owens, shaken, a reddened scrape on one cheekbone, said, "What happened?"

"For God's sake, never mind that. How is Benes?"

"He's hurt."

"Is he alive?"

"Yes. Help me."

Together they half lifted, half pulled Benes from the car. Benes' eyes were open but glazed, and he made only incoherent little sounds.

"How are you, professor?"

Owens said in a quick, low voice, "His head cracked hard against the door handle. Concussion, probably. But he *is* Benes. That's certain."

Gonder shouted, "We know that *now*, you . . ." He swallowed the last word with difficulty.

The door to the first limousine was opened. Together they lifted Benes in as a rifle shot cracked from somewhere above. Gonder threw himself into the car on top of Benes.

"Let's get the show out of here," he yelled.

The car and half the motorcycle escort moved on. The remainder stayed behind. Policemen ran for the building from which the rifle shot had sounded. The dying light of the burning kamikaze car cast a hellish glow on the scene. There was the rustle in the distance of the beginnings of a gathering crowd.

Gonder cradled Benes' head on his lap. The scientist was completely unconscious now, his breathing slow, his pulse feeble. Gonder stared earnestly at the man who might well be dead at any moment and muttered despairingly to himself, "We were almost there — almost there!"

CHAPTER 3 HEADQUARTERS

GRANT WAS only dopily aware of the hammering at his door. He stumbled upright and emerged from his bedroom, walking flat-footedly across the cold floor, and yawning prodigiously.

"Coming." He felt drugged and he *wanted* to feel drugged. In the way of business, he was trained to come alive at any extraneous noise. Instant alertness. Take a mass of sleep, add a pinch of thump and there would be an instant and vast flowering of *qui vive.*

But now he happened to be on his own time and to hell with it.

"What do you want?"

"From the colonel, sir," came from the other side of the door. "Open at once."

Against his will, Grant jolted into wakefulness. He stepped to one side of the door and flattened against the wall. He then opened the door as far as the chain would allow and said, "Shove your I.D. card here."

A card was thrust at him and he took it into his bedroom. He groped for his wallet and pinched out his Identifier. He inserted the card and read the result on the translucent screen.

He brought it back and unhinged the chain, ready, despite himself, for the appearance of a gun or for some sign of hostility. But the young man who entered looked completely harmless. "You'll have to come with me, sir, to headquarters."

"What time is it?"

"About 6:45, sir."

"A.M.?"

"Yes, sir."

"Damn it, why do they need me this time of day?"

"I can't say, sir. I'm following orders. I must ask you to come with me. Sorry." He tried a wry joke. "I didn't want to get up myself, but here I am."

"Do I have time to shave and shower?"

"Well — "

"All right then, do I have time to dress?"

"Yes, sir . . . but quickly!"

Grant scraped at the stubble along the angle of his jaw with his thumb and was glad he had showered the night before. "Give me five minutes for clothes and necessities."

He called out from the bathroom, "What's it all about?"

"I don't know, sir."

"What headquarters are we going to?"

"I don't think . . ."

"Never mind." The sound of rushing water made further speech impossible for a moment.

Grant emerged, feeling somberly semi-civilized. "But we're going to headquarters. You said that, right?"

"Yes, sir."

"All right, son," said Grant, pleasantly, "but if I think you're about to cross me, I'll cut you in two."

"Yes, sir."

*

Grant frowned when the car stopped. The dawn was gray and dank. There was a hint of forthcoming rain, the area was a run-down melange of warehouses and a quarter-mile back they had passed a roped-off area.

"What happened here?" Grant had asked and his companion was the usual mine of non-information.

Now they stopped and Grant gently placed his hand on the butt of his holstered revolver.

"You'd better tell me what happens next."

"We're here. This is a secret government installation. It doesn't look it, but it is."

The young man got out and so did the driver. "Please stay in the car, Mr. Grant."

The two stepped away for a hundred feet, while Grant looked warily about. There was a sudden jerk of movement and for a split second he was thrown off balance. Recovering, he began to fling the car door open, then hesitated in astonishment as smooth walls grew upward all about him.

It took him a moment to realize that he was sinking along with the car, that the car had been sitting on the top of an elevator shaft. By the time he had drunk that in, it was too late to try to get out.

Overhead a lid moved into place, and for a while Grant was in complete darkness. He flicked on the car's headlights but they splashed uselessly back from the round curve of the rising wall.

There was nothing to do but wait for an interminable three minutes, and then the car stopped.

Two large doors opened, and Grant's tensed muscles were ready for action. He called them off at once. A two-man scooter bearing one M.P. — one obvious M.P. in a completely legitimate military uniform — was waiting for him. On his helmet were the letters CMDF. On the scooter were the same letters.

Automatically, Grant put words to the initials. "Centralized Mountain Defense Forces," he muttered. "Coastal Marine Department Fisheries."

"What?" he said aloud. He had not heard the M.P.'s remark.

"If you'll get in, sir," repeated the M.P. with stiff propriety, indicating the empty seat.

"Sure. Quite a place you have here."

"Yes, sir."

"How big is it?"

They were passing through a cavernous, empty area, with trucks and motor carts lined against the wall, each with its CMDF insigne.

"Pretty big," said the M.P.

"That's what I like about everybody here," said Grant. "Full of priceless nuggets of data."

The scooter moved smoothly up a ramp to a higher level, a well-populated one. Uniformed individuals, both male and female, moved about busily, and there was an indefinable but undeniable air of agitation about the place. Grant caught himself watching a girl in what looked like a nurse's uniform (CMDF neatly printed over the curve of one breast) and he remembered the plans he had begun to make the evening before.

If this was another assignment . . .

The scooter made a sharp turn and stopped before a desk.

The M.P. scrambled out. "Charles Grant, sir."

The officer behind the desk was unmoved at the information. "Name?" he said.

"Charles Grant," said Grant, "like the nice man said."

"I.D. card, please."

Grant handed it over. It carried an embossed number only, to which the officer gave one curt glance. He inserted it into the Identifier on his desk, while Grant watched without much interest. It was precisely like his own wallet Identifier, overgrown and acromegalous. The gray, featureless screen lit up with his own portrait, full-face and profile, looking, as it always did in Grant's own eyes, darkly and menacingly gangsterish.

Where was the open, frank look? Where the charming smile? Where the dimples in his cheeks that drove the girls mad, mad? Only those dark, lowering eyebrows remained to give him that angry look. It was a wonder anyone recognized him.

The officer did, and apparently without trouble—one glance at the photo, one at Grant. The I.D. card was whipped out, handed back, and he was waved on.

The scooter turned right, passed through an archway and then down a long corridor, marked off for traffic, two lanes each way. Traffic was heavy, too, and Grant was the only one not uniformed.

Doors repeated themselves at almost hypnotically periodic intervals on either side, with pedestrian lanes immediately adjacent to the walls. Those were less heavily populated.

The scooter approached another archway, over which was a sign reading "Medical Division."

An M.P. on duty in a raised box like that of a traffic policeman hit a switch. Heavy steel doors opened and the scooter slid through and came to a stop.

Grant wondered what part of the city he was under by now.

The man in the general's uniform who was approaching hastily looked familiar. Grant placed him just before they had closed to within hand-shaking distance.

"Carter, isn't it? We met on the Transcontinental a couple of years ago. You weren't in uniform then."

"Hello, Grant. Oh, damn the uniform. I wear it only for status in this place. It's the only way we can establish a chain of command. Come with me. Granite Grant, wasn't it?"

"Oh, well."

They passed through a door into what was obviously an operating room. Grant glanced out through the observation window to see the usual sight of men and women in white, bustling about in almost visible asepsis, surrounded by the hard gleam of metalware, sharp and cold; and all of it dwarfed and rendered insignificant by the proliferation of electronic instruments that had converted medicine into a branch of engineering.

An operating table was being wheeled in, and a full shock of grizzled hair streamed out over the white pillow.

It was then that Grant had his worst stab of surprise.

"Benes?" he whispered.

"Benes," said General Carter, bleakly.

"What happened to him?"

"They got to him after all. Our fault. We live in an electronic age, Grant. Everything we do, we do with our transistorized servants in hand. Every enemy we have, we ward off by manipulating an electron flow. We had the route bugged in every possible way, but only for electronified enemies. We didn't count on an automobile with a man at the controls and on rifles with men at the triggers."

"I suppose you got none of them alive."

"None. The man in the car died on the spot. The others were killed by our bullets. We lost a few ourselves."

Grant looked down again. There was the look of emptiness on Benes' face that one associated with deep sedation.

"I assume he's alive so that there's hope."

"He's alive. But there isn't much hope."

Grant said, "Did anyone have a chance to talk to him?"

"A Captain Owens — William Owens — do you know him?"

Grant shook his head. "Just a glance at the airport at someone Gonder referred to by that name."

Carter said, "Owens spoke to Benes but got no crucial information. Gonder spoke to him. *You* spoke to him more than anyone. Did he tell you anything?"

"No, sir. I would not have understood if he had. It was my mission to get him into this country and nothing more."

"Of course. But you talked to him and he might have said more than he meant to."

"If he did, it went right over my head. But I don't think he did. Living on the Other Side, you get practice keeping your mouth shut."

Carter scowled. "Don't be unnecessarily superior, Grant. You get the same practice on this side. If you don't know that — I'm sorry, that was unnecessary."

"It's all right, General." Grant shrugged it off, tonelessly.

"Well, the point is, he talked to no one. He was put out of action before we could get what we wanted out of him. He might as well never have left the Other Side."

Grant said, "Coming here, I passed a place cordoned off . . ."

"That was the place. Five more blocks and we would have had him safe."

"What's wrong with him now?"

"Brain injury. We have to operate — and that's why we need you."

"*Me?*" Grant said, strenuously. "Listen, General, at brain surgery, I'm a child. I flunked Advanced Cerebellum at old State U."

Carter did not react and to Grant his own words sounded hollow.

"Come with me," said Carter.

Grant followed, through a door, down a short stretch of corridor, and into another room.

"Central Monitoring," said Carter, briefly. The walls were covered with TV panels. The central chair was half-surrounded by a semicircular console of switches, banked on a steep incline.

Carter sat down while Grant remained standing.

Carter said, "Let me give you the essence of the situation. You understand there's a stalemate between Ourselves and Them."

"And has been for a long time. Of course."

"The stalemate isn't a bad thing, altogether. We compete; we run scared all the time; and we get a lot done that way. Both of us. But if the stalemate must break, it's got to break in favor of our side. You see that, I suppose?"

"I think I do, General," said Grant, dryly.

"Benes represents the possibility of such a break. If he could tell us what he knows . . ."

"May I ask a question, sir?"

"Go ahead."

"*What* does he know? What sort of thing?"

"Not yet. Not yet. Just wait a few moments. The exact nature of the information is not crucial at the moment. Let me continue. If he could tell us what he knows, then the stalemate breaks on our side. If he died; or even if he recovers but without being able to give us our information because of brain damage, then the stalemate continues."

Grant said, "Aside from humanitarian sorrow for the loss of a great mind, we can say that maintaining the stalemate isn't too bad."

"Yes, if the situation is just as I have described, but it may not be."

"How do you make that out?"

"Consider Benes. He is known as a moderate but we had no indication that he was having trouble with his government. He had shown every sign of being loyal for a quarter of a century, and he'd been well treated. Now he suddenly defects . . ."

"Because he wants to break the stalemate on our side."

"Does he? Or could it be that he revealed enough of his work, before realizing its full significance, to give the Other Side the key to the advance. He may then have come to realize that, without quite meaning to, he had placed world dominion securely into the hands of his own side, and perhaps he wasn't sufficiently confident in the virtues of his own side to be satisfied with that. So now he comes to us, not so much to give us the victory, as to give no one the victory. He comes to us in order to maintain the stalemate."

"Is there any evidence for that, sir?"

"Not one bit," said Carter. "But you see it as a possibility, I presume, and you realize that there is not one bit of evidence against it, either."

"Go on."

"If the matter of life or death for Benes meant a choice between total victory for us or continued stalemate — well, we could manage. To lose our chance of total victory would be a damned shame, but we might get another chance tomorrow. However, what might be facing us is a choice between stalemate and total defeat, and there one of the alternatives is completely unbearable. Do you agree?"

"Of course."

"You see, then, that if there is even a small possibility that Benes' death will involve us in total defeat, then that death must be prevented at any price, at any cost, at any risk."

"I take it you mean that statement for my benefit, General, because you're going to ask me to do something. As it happens, I've risked my life to prevent eventualities considerably short of total defeat. I've never really enjoyed it, if you want a confession, but I've done it. However, what can I do in the operating room? When I needed a band-aid over my short ribs yesterday, Benes had to put it on for me. And compared to other aspects of medical technique, I'm very good at band-aids."

Carter didn't react to that, either. "Gonder recommended you for this. On general principles, in the first place. He considers you a remarkably capable man. So do I."

"General, I don't need the flattery. I find it irritating."

"Damn it, man. I'm not flattering you. I'm explaining something. Gonder considers you capable in general, but more than that, he considers your mission incomplete. You were to get Benes to us safely, and that has not been done."

"He was safe when I was relieved by Gonder himself."

"Nevertheless, he is not safe now."

"Are you appealing to my professional pride, General?"

"If you like."

"All right. I'll hold the scalpels. I'll wipe the perspiration from the surgeon's forehead. I'll even wink at the nurses. I think that's the complete list of my competencies in an operating room."

"You won't be alone. You'll be part of a team."

"I somehow expect that," said Grant. "Someone else will have to aim the scalpels and push them. I just hold them in a tray."

Carter manipulated a few switches with a sure touch. On one TV screen, a pair of figures in dark glasses came into instant view. They were bent intently over a laser beam, its red light narrowing to threadlike thinness. The light flashed out and they removed their glasses.

Carter said, "That's Peter Duval. Have you ever heard of him?"

"Sorry, but no."

"He's the top brain surgeon in the country."

"Who's the girl?"

"She assists him."

"Hah!"

"Don't be single-tracked. She's an extremely competent technician."

Grant wilted a bit. "I'm sure of it, sir."

"You say you saw Owens at the airport?"

"Very briefly, sir."

"He'll be with you, too. Also our chief of the Medical Section. He'll brief you."

Another quick manipulation and this time the TV screen came on with that low buzz that signified two-way sound attachment.

An amiable bald head at close quarters dwarfed the intricate network of a circulatory system that filled the wall behind.

Carter said, "Max!"

Michaels looked up. His eyes narrowed. He looked rather washed out. "Yes, Al."

"Grant is ready for you. Hurry it on. There isn't much time."

"There certainly isn't. I'll come get him." For a moment, Michaels caught Grant's eye. He said, slowly, "I hope you're prepared, Mr. Grant, for the most unusual experience of your life. Or of anyone's."

CHAPTER 4 BRIEFING

IN MICHAELS' OFFICE, Grant found himself looking open-mouthed at the map of the circulatory system.

Michaels said, "It's an unholy mess, but it's a map of the territory. Every mark on it is a road; every junction is a cross-road. That map is as intricate as a road map of the United States. More so, for it's in three dimensions."

"Good lord!"

"A hundred thousand miles of blood vessels. You see very little of it now; most of it is microscopic and won't be visible to you without considerable magnification, but put it all together in a single line and it would go four times around the Earth or, if you prefer, nearly halfway to the Moon. Have you had any sleep, Grant?"

"About six hours. I napped on the plane, too. I'm in good shape."

"Good, you'll have a chance to eat and shave and tend to other such matters if necessary. I wish I had slept." He held up a hand as soon as he had said that. "Not that I'm in bad shape. I'm not complaining. Have you ever taken a morphogen?"

"Never heard of it. Is it some kind of drug?"

"Yes. Relatively new. It's not the sleep you need, you know. One doesn't rest in sleep to any greater extent than one would by stretching out comfortably with the eyes open. Less, maybe. It's the dreams we need. We've got to have dreaming time, otherwise cerebral coordination breaks down and you begin to have hallucinations and, eventually, death."

"The morphogen makes you dream? Is that it?"

"Exactly. It knocks you out for half an hour of solid dreaming and then you're set for the day. Take my advice, though, and stay away from the stuff unless it's an emergency."

"Why? Does it leave you tired?"

"No. Not particularly tired. It's just that the dreams are bad. The morphogen vacuums the mind; cleans out the mental garbage accumulated during the day; and it's quite an experience. Don't do it. I had no choice. That map had to be prepared and I spent all night at it."

"That map?"

"It's Benes' system to the last capillary and I've had to learn all I could concerning it. Up here, almost centrally located in the cranium, right near the pituitary, is the blood clot."

"Is that the problem?"

"It certainly is. Everything else can be handled. The general bruises and contusions, the shock, the concussion. The clot can't be, not without surgery. And quickly."

"How long has he got, Dr. Michaels?"

"Can't say. It won't be fatal, we hope, for quite a while, but brain damage will come long before death does. And for this organization, brain damage will be as bad as death. The people here expect miracles from our Benes and now they've been badly rattled. Carter, in particular, has had a bad blow and wants you."

Grant said, "You mean he expects the Other Side will try again."

"He doesn't say so, but I suspect that's what he fears and why he wants you on the team."

Grant looked about. "Is there any reason to think this place has been penetrated? Have they planted agents here?"

"Not to my knowledge, but Carter is a suspicious man. I think he suspects the possibility of medical assassination."

"Duval?"

Michaels shrugged. "He's an unpopular character and the instrument he uses can cause death if it slips a hairbreadth."

"How can he be stopped?"

"He can't."

"Then use someone else; someone you can trust."

"No one else has the necessary skill. And Duval is right here with us. And, after all, there is no proof that he isn't completely loyal."

"But if I'm placed near Duval as a male nurse and if I am assigned the task of watching him closely, I will do no good. I won't know what he's doing; or whether he's doing it honestly and correctly. In fact, I tell you that when he opens the skull, I'll probably pass out."

"He won't open the skull," said Michaels. "The clot can't be reached from outside. He's definite about that."

"But, then . . ."

"We'll reach it from the inside."

Grant frowned. Slowly, he shook his head. "You know, I don't know what the hell you're talking about."

Michaels said, quietly, "Mr. Grant, everyone else engaged in this project knows the score, and understands exactly what he or she is to do. You're the outsider and it is rather a chore to have to educate you. Still, if I must, I must. I'm going to have to acquaint you with some of the theoretical work done in this institution."

Grant's lip quirked. "Sorry, Doctor, but you've just said a naughty word. At college, I majored in football with a strong minor in girls. Don't waste theory on me."

"I have seen your record, Mr. Grant, and it is not quite as you say. However, I will not deprive you of your manhood by accusing you of your obvious intelligence and education, even if we are in private. I will not waste theory on you, but will get the nub of the information to you without that. I assume you have observed our insigne, CMDF."

"Sure have."

"Do you have any idea of what it means?"

"I've made a few guesses. How about Consolidated Martian Dimwits and Fools? I've got a better one than that but it's unprintable."

"It happens to stand for Combined Miniature Deterrent Forces."

"That makes less sense than my suggestion," said Grant.

"I'll explain. Have you ever heard of the miniaturization controversy?"

Grant thought a while. "I was in college then. We spent a couple of sessions on it in the physics course."

"In between football games?"

"Yes. In the off season, as a matter of fact. If I remember it, a group of physicists claimed they could reduce the size of objects to any degree, and it was exposed as a fraud. Well, maybe not a fraud but a mistake anyway. I remember the class ran through several arguments showing why it was impossible to reduce a man to the size of, say, a mouse, and keep him a man."

"I'm sure this was done in every college in the land. Do you remember any of the objections?"

"I think so. If you're going to reduce size you can do it in one of two ways. You can push the individual atoms of an object closer together; or you can discard a certain proportion of the atoms altogether. To push the atoms together against the inter-atomic repulsive forces would take extraordinary pressures. The pressures at the center of Jupiter would be insufficient to compress a man to the size of a mouse. Am I right so far?"

"You are luminous as the day."

"And even if you managed it, the pressure would kill anything alive. Aside from that, an object reduced in size by pushing atoms together would retain all its original mass, and an object the size of a mouse with the mass of a man would be difficult to handle."

"Amazing, Mr. Grant. You must have amused your girl friends for many hours with this romantic talk. And the other method?"

"The other method is to remove atoms in careful ratio so that the mass and size of an object decreases while the relationship of the parts remains constant. Only if you reduce a man to the size of a mouse you can keep only one atom out of maybe seventy thousand. If you do that to the brain, what is left is scarcely more complicated than the brain of a mouse in the first place. Besides, how do you re-expand the object, as the miniaturizing physicists claimed to be able to do? How do you get the atoms back and put them in their right places?"

"Quite so, Mr. Grant. But then how did some reputable physicists come to think that miniaturization was practical?"

"I don't know, doctor, but you don't hear of it any more."

"Partly because the colleges did such a careful job, under orders, of knocking it on the head. The technique went underground both here and on the Other Side. Literally. Here. Underground." It was almost with passion that Michaels tapped the desk before him. "And we must maintain special courses in miniaturization techniques for graduate physicists who can learn it nowhere else, except in analogous schools on the Other Side. Miniaturization is quite possible, but by neither method you have described. Have you ever seen a photograph enlarged, Mr. Grant? Or reduced to microfilm size?"

"Of course."

"Without theory, then, I tell you that the same process can be used on three-dimensional objects; even on a man. We are miniaturized, not as literal objects, but as images; as three-dimensional images manipulated from outside the universe of space-time."

Grant smiled. "Now, teacher, those are just words."

"Yes, but you don't want theory, do you? What physicists discovered ten years ago was the utilization of hyper-space, a space, that is, of more than the three ordinary spatial dimensions. The concept is beyond grasping; the mathematics are almost beyond grasp; but the funny part is that it can be done. Objects can be miniaturized. We neither get rid of atoms nor push them together. We reduce the size of the atoms, too; we reduce everything; and the mass decreases automatically. When we wish, we restore the size."

"You sound serious," said Grant. "Are you telling me that we can really reduce a man to the size of a mouse?"

"In principle we can reduce a man to the size of a bacterium, of a virus, of an atom. There is no theoretical limit to the amount of miniaturization. We can shrink an army with all its men and equipment to a size that will fit in a match box. Ideally, we could then ship that match box where it is needed and put the army into business after restoring it to full size. You see the significance?"

Grant said, "And the Other Side can do it, too, I take it."

"We're certain they can — but come, Grant. Matters are progressing at full speed and our time is limited. Come with me."

*

It was "come with me" here and "come with me" there. Since Grant had awakened that morning, he had not been allowed to remain in one place for longer than fifteen minutes. It annoyed him and yet there seemed nothing he could do about it. Was it a deliberate attempt to keep him from having time enough to think? What were they preparing to spring on him?

He and Michaels were in the scooter now, Michaels handling it like a veteran.

"If both We and They have it, we neutralize each other," said Grant.

"Yes, but in addition," said Michaels, "it does neither of us very much good. There's a catch."

"Oh?"

"We've worked for ten years to extend the size ratio, to reach greater intensities of miniaturization, and of expansion, too — just a matter of reversing the hyper-field. Unfortunately, we've reached our theoretical limits in this direction."

"What are they?"

"Not very favorable. The Uncertainty Principle intervenes. Extent of miniaturization multiplied by the duration of miniaturization, using the proper units, of course, is equal to an expression containing Planck's constant. If a man is reduced to half-size, he can be kept so for centuries. If he is reduced to mousesize, that can be kept up for days. If he is reduced to bacterium-size, he can be kept up only for hours. After that he expands again."

"But then he can be miniaturized again."

"Only after a sizable lag period. Do you want some of the mathematical background?"

"No. I'll take your word for everything."

They had arrived at the foot of an escalator. Michaels, with a small, weary grunt, got out of the scooter. Grant vaulted the side.

He leaned against the railing as the staircase moved majestically upward. "And what has Benes got?"

"They tell me he claims he can beat the Uncertainty Principle. Supposedly, he knows how to maintain miniaturization indefinitely."

"You don't sound as though you believe that."

Michaels shrugged. "I am skeptical. If he extends both miniaturization intensity and miniaturization duration, that can only be at the expense of something else, but for the life of me I can't imagine what that something else might be. Perhaps that only means I am not a Benes. In any case, he says he can do it and we cannot take the chance of not believing him. Neither can the Other Side, so they've tried to kill him."

They had come to the top of the escalator and Michaels had paused there briefly to complete his remark. Now he moved back to take a second escalator up another floor.

"Now, Grant, you can understand what we must do: save Benes. Why we must do it: for the information he has. And how we must do it: by miniaturization."

"Why by miniaturization?"

"Because the brain clot cannot be reached from outside. I told you that. So we will miniaturize a submarine, inject it into an artery, and with Captain Owens at the controls and with myself as pilot, journey to the clot. There, Duval and his assistant, Miss Peterson, will operate."

Grant's eyes opened wide. "And I?"

"You will be along as a member of the crew. General supervision, apparently."

Grant said, violently, "Not I. I am not volunteering for any such thing. Not for a minute."

He turned and started walking down the up-escalator, with little effect. Michaels followed him, sounding amused. "It is your business to take risks, isn't it?"

"Risks of my own choosing. Risks I am used to. Risks I am prepared for. Give me as much time to think of miniaturization as you have had and I'll take the risk."

"My dear Grant. You have not been asked to volunteer. It

is my understanding that you have been assigned to this duty. And now its importance has been explained to you. After all, I am going too, and I am not as young as you, nor have I ever been a football player. In fact, I'll tell you, I was depending on you to keep my courage up by coming along, since courage is your business."

"If so, I'm a rotten businessman," muttered Grant. Irrelevantly, almost petulantly, he said, "I want coffee."

He stood still and let the escalator carry him up again. Near the top of the escalator was a door marked "Conference Room." They entered.

Grant grew aware of the contents of the room in stages. What he saw first was that one end of the long table that filled the center of the room was a multi-cup coffee dispenser and that next to it was a tray of sandwiches.

He moved toward that end of the table at once and it was only after downing half a cup of coffee, hot and black, and following that by a Grant-sized bite at a sandwich, that item two entered his awareness.

This was Duval's assistant — Miss Peterson, wasn't that her name? — looking down-in-the-mouth but very beautiful and standing terribly close to Duval. Grant had the instant feeling that he was going to find it difficult to like the surgeon, and only then did he begin to absorb the rest of the room.

A colonel sat at one end of the table, looking annoyed. One hand twirled an ashtray slowly while the ashes of his cigarette dropped to the floor. He said emphatically to Duval, "I've made my attitude quite clear."

Grant recognized Captain Owens standing under the portrait of the president. The eagerness and smiles he had seen at the airport were gone and there was a bruise on one cheekbone. He looked nervous and upset and Grant sympathized with the sensation.

"Who's the colonel?" Grant asked Michaels in a low voice.

"Donald Reid, my opposite number on the military side of the fence."

"I take it he's annoyed with Duval."

"Constantly. He's got a lot of company. Few like him."

Grant had the impulse to answer, *She* seems to, but the words sounded petty in his thoughts and he dismissed them. Lord, what a dish! What did she see in that solemn cutthroat?

Reid was talking in a low voice, carefully controlled. "And aside from that, Doctor, what is *she* doing here?"

"Miss Cora Peterson," said Duval, icily, "is my assistant. Where I go professionally, she accompanies me professionally."

"This is a dangerous mission . . ."

"And Miss Peterson has volunteered, understanding full well its dangers."

"A number of men, entirely qualified to help, have also volunteered. Matters would be far less complicated if one of those men accompanied you. I will assign you one."

"You will not assign me one, Colonel, for if you do, I will not go, and there will be no power to make me. Miss Peterson is a third and fourth arm to me. She knows my requirements well enough to do her job without instructions, to be there before I call, to supply what is needed without being asked. I will *not* take a stranger who will need to be shouted at. I can *not* be responsible for success if I lose one second because my technician and I do not mesh, and I will *not* take any assignment in which I am not given a free hand with which to arrange matters in such a way as will carry with it the best chance for success."

Grant's eye moved to Cora Peterson again. She looked acutely embarrassed, yet stared at Duval with the expression Grant had once seen in a beagle's eye when its little-boy-owner returned from school. Grant found that intensely annoying.

Michaels' voice cut across the argument as Reid was rising furiously to his feet. "I would suggest, Don, that since the key step of the entire operation rests upon Dr. Duval's hand and eye and since, in fact, we cannot now dictate to him, we humor him in this respect — without prejudice to necessary action afterward, eh? I am willing to take responsibility for that."

He was offering Reid a face-saving way out, Grant realized, and Reid, fuming darkly, would have to take it.

Reid slammed the flat of his hand on the table before him. "All right. Let it be on record that I opposed this." He sat back, lips trembling.

Duval sat down also, unconcerned. Grant moved forward to pull out a chair for Cora, but she helped herself and was seated before he could reach her.

Michaels said, "Dr. Duval, this is Grant, a young man who will be accompanying us."

"As muscle man, Doctor," said Grant. "My only qualification."

Duval looked up cursorily. His acknowledgement was a minimal nod thrown in Grant's general direction.

"And Miss Peterson."

Grant smiled flashily. She smiled not at all and said, "How do you do?"

"Hello," said Grant, looked down at what little was left of his second sandwich, realized that no one else was eating at all, and put it down.

Carter came in at this point, walking rapidly and nodding vaguely to right and left. He sat down and said, "Will you join us, Captain Owens? Grant?"

Owens reluctantly moved to the table and took his place opposite Duval. Grant sat down several chairs removed and found himself able, in looking at Carter, to contemplate Cora's face in profile.

Could a job be entirely bad if *she* were part of it?

Michaels, who sat down immediately next to Grant, leaned forward to whisper in his ear. "It isn't a bad idea to have a woman along. The men, perhaps, will be more on their mettle. And it would please me."

"Is that why you made the pitch for her?"

"No. Duval is serious. He wouldn't go without her."

"Is he that dependent on her?"

"Perhaps not. But he's that intent on having his way. Especially against Reid. No love lost there."

Carter said, "To business. You can drink, or eat, if you wish, while this is going on. Do any of you have any urgent point to make?"

Grant said, suddenly, "I haven't volunteered, general. I decline the post and suggest you find a substitute."

"You're not a volunteer, Grant, and your offer to decline is declined. Gentlemen — and Miss Peterson — Mr. Grant has been chosen to accompany the expedition for a variety of reasons. For one thing, it was he who brought Benes to this country, managing that assignment with complete skill."

All eyes turned to Grant, who felt himself wincing at the momentary expectation that there would be a polite patter of applause. There was none, and he relaxed.

Carter went on. "He is a communications expert and an experienced frogman. He has a record of resourcefulness and flexibility and is professionally capable of making instant decisions. For that reason I will place the power of making policy decisions in his hands once the voyage begins. Is that understood?"

It apparently was, and Grant, staring in annoyance at his fingertips, said, "Apparently it is up to the rest of you to do your jobs while I take care of emergencies. I am sorry but I wish to state for the record that I do not consider myself qualified for this post."

"The statement is recorded," said Carter, unembarrassed, "and we will go on. Captain Owens has designed an experimental submarine for oceanographic research. It is not ideally suited for the task at hand, but it is itself at hand, and there is no other vessel in existence that is better suited. Owens himself will, of course, be at the controls of his ship, the *Proteus*.

"Dr. Michaels will be the pilot. He has prepared and studied the map of Benes' circulatory system, which we will shortly consider. Dr. Duval and his assistant will be in charge of the actual operation, the removal of the clot.

"You all know the importance of this mission. We hope for a successful operation and for your safe return. There is the chance that Benes may die during the operation, but that becomes a certainty if the mission is not undertaken. There is a chance that the ship may be lost, but under the circumstances, I am afraid that ship and crew are expendable. The possible price is large but the gain we seek — I don't mean the CMDF only, but all mankind — is greater."

Grant muttered under his breath, "Yea, team."

Cora Peterson caught it and looked at him with brief penetration from under dark eyelashes. Grant flushed.

Carter said, "Show them the chart, Michaels."

Michaels pressed a button on the instrument before him and the wall lit up with the tri-dimensional map of Benes' circulatory system that Grant had last seen in Michaels' office. It seemed to rush toward them and enlarge as Michaels turned a knob. What was left of the circulatory network made up the clear delineation of a head and neck.

The blood vessels stood out with an almost fluorescent brilliance and then grid lines appeared across it. A thin, dark arrow darted into the field, manipulated by the photo-pointer in Michaels' hand. Michaels did not rise but remained seated in his chair, one arm over its back.

"The clot," he said, "is there." It had not been visible to Grant's eyes, at least until it had been pointed out, but now that the black arrow delicately marked out its limits, Grant could see it, a small, solid nodule plugging an arteriole.

"It represents no immediate danger to life, but this section of the brain" (the arrow danced about) "is suffering from nerve-compression and may already have experienced damage. Dr. Duval tells me that the effects may be irreversible in twelve hours or less. An attempt to operate in the ordinary manner will involve cutting through the skull either here, here, or here. In each of these three cases, unavoidable damage will be extensive and the results doubtful.

"On the other hand, we could attempt to reach the clot via the blood stream. If we can enter the carotid artery here in the neck, we will be on a reasonably direct route to our destination." The flowing of the arrow along the line of the red artery, picking its way through the blueness of the veins, made it seem very easy.

Michaels went on, "If, then, the *Proteus* and its crew are miniaturized and injected . . ."

Owens spoke up suddenly. "Wait a while." His voice was harsh and metallic. "How far will we be reduced?"

"We'll have to be small enough to avoid activating the body's defenses. The overall length of the ship will be three micra."

"How much is that in inches?" interjected Grant.

"Just under a ten-thousandth of an inch. The ship will be about the size of a large bacterium."

"Well, then," said Owens. "If we enter an artery, we will be exposed to the full force of the arterial current."

"Not quite a mile an hour," said Carter.

"Never mind the miles per hour. We will be moving about one hundred thousand times the length of our ship each second. That will be equivalent, under ordinary circumstances, to moving two hundred miles a second—or something like that. On our miniaturized scale we'll be moving a dozen times as fast as any astronaut ever moved. At least."

"Undoubtedly," said Carter, "but what of it? Every red

blood corpuscle in the blood stream moves as quickly and the ship is much more sturdily built than the corpuscle."

"No, it is *not,*" said Owens, passionately. "A red blood corpuscle contains billions of atoms, but the *Proteus* will crowd billions of billions of billions of atoms into the same space; miniaturized atoms, to be sure, but what of that? We will be made up of an immensely larger number of units than the red blood corpuscle and we'll be flabbier for that reason. Furthermore, the red blood corpuscle is in an environment of atoms equal in size to those that make it up; we will be in an environment made up of what will be to us monstrous atoms."

Carter said, "Can you answer that, Max?"

Michaels harumphed. "I do not pretend to be as expert on the problems of miniaturization as Captain Owens. I suspect that he is thinking of the report by James and Schwartz that fragility increases with intensity of miniaturization."

"Exactly," said Owens.

"The increase is a slow one, if you remember, and James and Schwartz had to make some simplifying assumptions in the course of their analysis which may prove to be not entirely valid. After all, when we enlarge objects, they certainly do not become *less* fragile."

"Oh, come on, we've never enlarged any object more than a hundred fold," said Owens, contemptuously, "and here we are talking about miniaturizing a ship about a million times in linear dimensions. No one's ever gone that far, or even anything close to that far, in either direction. The fact is that there isn't anyone in the world who can predict just how fragile we will become, or how well we can stand up to the pounding of the blood stream, or even how we might respond to the action of a white blood corpuscle. Isn't that so, Michaels?"

Michaels said, "Well, yes."

Carter said, with what seemed rising impatience, "It would seem that the course of orderly experiment leading to so drastic a miniaturization has not yet been completed. We're in no position to carry through a program of such experimentation so we have to take our chances. If the ship does not survive, it doesn't."

"That bucks me up," muttered Grant.

Cora Peterson leaned toward him, whispering tightly, "Please, Mr. Grant, you're not on the football field."

"Oh, you know my record, miss?"

"Shh."

Carter said, "We are taking all the precautions we can. Benes will be in deep hypothermia for his own sake. By freezing him we will cut down the oxygen requirements of the brain. That will mean the heartbeat will be drastically slowed and the velocity of the blood flow as well."

Owens said, "Even so, I doubt that we could survive the turbulence . . ."

Michaels said, "Captain, if you stay away from the artery walls, you will be in the region of laminar flow — no turbulence to speak of. We will be in the artery only for minutes, and once in the smaller vessels we will have no problem. The only place where we would not be able to avoid killing turbulence would be in the heart itself and we would go nowhere near the heart. May I continue, now?"

"Please do," said Carter.

"Having reached the clot, it will be destroyed by a laser beam. The laser and its beam, having been miniaturized in proportion, will not, if properly used — as in Duval's hands it is sure to be — do any damage to the brain or even the blood vessel itself. Nor will it be necessary to demolish every vestige of the clot. It will be enough to break it up into fragments. The white blood cells will then take care of it.

"We will leave the vicinity at once, of course, returning by way of the venous system, until we reach the base of the neck, where we will be removed from the jugular vein."

Grant said, "How will anyone know where we are and when?"

Carter said, "Michaels will pilot you and see to it that you are in the right place at all times. You will be in communication with us by radio . . ."

"You don't know if that will work," put in Owens. "There's a problem in adapting the radio waves across the miniaturization gap, and no one has ever tried this big a gap."

"True, but we will try. In addition, the *Proteus* is nuclear powered and we will be able to trace its radioactivity, also across the gap. You will have just sixty minutes, gentlemen."

Grant said, "You mean we have to complete the job and be out in sixty minutes?"

"Exactly sixty. Your size will have been adjusted to that. You will have ample time. If you stay for a longer interval, you will start enlarging automatically. We can keep you down no longer. If we had Benes' knowledge we could keep you down indefinitely, but if we had his knowledge . . ."

"This trip would be unnecessary," said Grant, sardonically.

"Exactly. And if you begin enlarging within Benes' body, you will become large enough to attract the attention of the body defenses, and shortly thereafter, you will kill Benes. You will see to it that this does not happen."

Carter then looked about. "Any further remarks? In that case, you will begin preparations. We'd like to make entry into Benes as quickly as possible."

CHAPTER 5 SUBMARINE

THE LEVEL of activity in the hospital room had reached the visual analog of a scream. Everyone was moving at a rapid walk, almost a half-run. Only the figure on the operating table was still. A heavy thermal blanket lay over it, the numerous coils snaking through filled with their circulating refrigerant. And under it was the nude body, chilled to the point where life within it was a sluggish whisper.

Benes' head was now shaven and marked off like a nautical chart in numbered lines of latitude and longitude. On his sleep-sunk face was a look of sadness, frozen deeply in.

On the wall behind him was another reproduction of the circulatory system, enlarged to the point where the chest, neck, and head were sufficient in themselves to cover the wall from end to end and floor to ceiling. It had become a forest in which the large vessels were as thick as a man's arm while the fine capillaries fuzzed all the spaces between.

In the control tower, brooding over the operation room, Carter and Reid watched. They could see the desk-level banks of monitors, at each of which a technician sat, each in his CMDF uniform, a symphony in zippered white.

Carter moved to the window, while Reid said softly into a mike, "Bring the *Proteus* into the miniaturization room."

It was customary protocol to give such orders in a quiet voice, and there was quiet on the floor. Last minute adjustments were being frantically made at the thermal blanket. Each technician studied his own monitor as though it were his new bride, isolated at last. The nurses hovered about Benes like large, starch-winged butterflies. With the *Proteus* beginning the preparation for miniaturization, every man and woman on the floor knew the last stage of the countdown had started.

Reid pushed a button. "Heart!"

The heart sector was laid out in detail on the TV screen that was rostrumed just under Reid. Within that sector, the EKG recordings dominated and the heartbeat sounded in a dull, double thump of sorrowful slowness. "How does it look, Henry?"

"Perfect. Holding steady at thirty-two per minute. No abnormalities, acoustic or electronic. The rest of him should only be like this."

"Good." Reid flicked him off. To a heart man, what could be wrong if the heart was right?

He turned on the lung sector. The world on the screen was suddenly one of respiration rates. "All right, Jack?"

"All right, Dr. Reid. I've got the respiration down to six per minute. Can't take it any lower."

"I'm not asking you to. Carry on."

Hypothermia next. This sector was larger than the rest. It had to concern itself with all the body and here the theme was the thermometer. Temperature readings at the limbs, at various points of the torso, at delicate contacts making readings at definite depths below the skin. There were constantly creeping temperature recordings, with each wiggle bearing its own label: "Circulatory," "Respiratory," "Cardiac," "Renal," "Intestinal," and so on.

"Any problems, Sawyer?" asked Reid.

"No, sir. Over-all average is at 28° C. — 82° F."

"You needn't convert, thank you."

"Yes, sir."

It was as though Reid could feel the hypothermia biting at his own vitals. Sixteen Fahrenheit degrees below normal; sixteen crucial degrees, slowing metabolism to about one-third normal; cutting the oxygen needs to one-third; slowing the heartbeat, the rate of blood flow, the scale of life, the strain on the clot-blocked brain — and making the environment more favorable for the ship that was soon to enter the jungle of the human interior.

Carter moved back toward Reid, "All set, Don?"

"As near as can be managed, considering that this was improvised overnight."

"I doubt that very much."

Reid flushed. "What's that supposed to mean, General?"

"No improvisation was needed. It's no secret to me that you've been laying the groundwork for biological experiments with miniaturization. Have you been planning, specifically, the exploration of the human circulatory system?"

"Not specifically, no. But my team has been working on such problems as a matter of course. That was their job."

"Don . . ." Carter hesitated, then went on tightly. "If this fails, Don, someone's head will be needed for the Congressional trophy room, and mine will be the handiest. If this succeeds, you and your men will come out of it smelling like lilies of the valley. Don't try to push that too far if it happens."

"The military will still have first call, eh? Are you telling me not to get in the way?"

"It might be sensible not to. Another thing. What's wrong with the girl, Cora Peterson?"

"Nothing. Why?"

"Your voice was loud enough. I heard you just before I came into the conference room. Do you know of any reason why she shouldn't be on board?"

"She's a woman. She may not be reliable in emergencies. Besides . . ."

"Yes?"

"If you want the truth, Duval assumed his usual I-am-the-law-and-the-prophets manner, and I automatically objected. How far do *you* trust Duval?"

"What do you mean, trust?"

"What's your real reason for sending Grant along on the mission? Who's he supposed to keep his eye on?"

Carter said in a low, husky tone, "I haven't told him to keep an eye on anyone. The crew should be about through in the sterilization corridor by now."

•

Grant sniffed at the faintly medicinal odor in the atmosphere and was grateful for the opportunity of a quick shave. The CMDF uniform wasn't bad, either; one piece, belted, and an odd cross between the scientific and the dashing. The one they had found for him bound him slightly under the armpits, but he'd only be wearing it for an hour.

In single file, he and the others of the crew passed down the corridor in dim light that was rich in ultraviolet. They wore dark goggles against the dangers of that radiation.

Cora Peterson walked immediately ahead of Grant. He silently deplored the darkness of the lenses before his eyes and the manner in which they dimmed the interesting style of her walk.

Wanting to make conversation, he said, "Is this walk-through really sufficient to sterilize us, Miss Peterson?"

She turned her head briefly and said, "I think you need have no masculine uneasiness."

Grant's mouth quirked. He had asked for that. He said, "You underestimate my naïveté, Miss Peterson, and I am unfairly run through by your sophistication."

"I didn't meant to offend you."

The door at the end of the corridor opened automatically and Grant, as automatically, closed the gap between them and offered his hand. She evaded it and stepped across at the heels of Duval.

Grant said, "No offense. But my meaning was that we aren't actually sterile. Microbe-wise, I mean. At best, it is only our surfaces that are sterile. Inside, we teem with germs."

"For that matter," Cora responded, "Benes isn't sterile, either. Microbe-wise, I mean. But every germ we kill is one less germ we might introduce. Our germs will be miniaturized with us, of course, and we don't know how such miniaturized germs will affect a human being if released in his blood stream. On the other hand, after one hour any miniaturized germs in his blood stream will expand to their normal size and that expansion might be harmful, for all we know. The less Benes is subjected to unknown factors, the better." She shook her head. "There's so much we don't know. This really isn't the way to experiment."

"But we have no choice, do we, Miss Peterson? And may I call you Cora, by the way, for the duration?"

"It makes no difference to me."

They had entered a large, round room glassed-in. It was floored completely in hexagonal tiles some three feet across, roughened into close-packed, semicircular bubbles, the whole made of some milk-white, glassy material. At the center of the room was a single tile, like the rest except that it was deep red.

Filling much of the room was a white vessel some fifty feet in length, horseshoe in shape, with an upper bubble the front of which was glassed in and which was topped by a smaller bubble, entirely transparent. It was on a hydraulic lift and was being maneuvered into the center of the room.

Michaels had moved up next to Grant. "The *Proteus*," he said. "Our home away from home for the next hour or so."

"This is a huge room," Grant said, looking about.

"It's our miniaturization room. It's been used for the miniaturization of artillery pieces and small atomic bombs. It can also serve to hold deminiaturized insects—you know, ants blown up to the size of locomotives for easy study. Such bio-experiments haven't been authorized yet, though we've sneaked in one or two quiet efforts along that line. They're putting the *Proteus* over Zero Module; that's the red one. Then, I suppose, we get in. Nervous, Mr. Grant?"

"And how! And you?"

Michaels nodded in rueful agreement. "And how!"

The *Proteus* had been adjusted onto its cradle now and the hydraulic lifts that had maneuvered it into place were drawn off. A ladder on one side led to the entrance.

The ship gleamed in sterile whiteness, from the featureless bluntness of its prow to the double jet and upright fin at the rear.

Owens said, "I'll get in first. When I signal, the rest of you come in." He moved up the ladder.

"It's his ship," muttered Grant. "Why not?" Then he said to Michaels, "He seems more nervous than we."

"That's just his way. He *looks* nervous all the time. And if he is, he has reason. He has a wife and two young daughters. Duval and his assistant are both single."

"I am, too," said Grant. "And you?"

"Divorced. No children. So you see."

Owens could be seen plainly, now, in the bubble-top. He seemed intent on objects immediately before him. Then he waved the come-in gesture. Michaels responded and moved up the ladder. Duval followed him. Grant motioned Cora to enter ahead of himself.

All were in their seats when Grant ducked through the small chamber that made up the hatch. Above, in the lone upper seat, was Owens at the controls. Below were four more seats. The two in the rear, well on either side, were occupied by Cora and Duval, Cora on the right near the ladder that led up to the bubble, Duval on the left. In the bow were the other two seats, close together. Michaels had already taken the one on the left. Grant sat down next to him.

On either side were workbenches and a set of what looked like auxiliary controls. Underneath the benches were cabinets. In the rear was a pair of small rooms, one a workroom, the other for storage.

It was still dark inside. Michaels said, "We will put you to work, Grant. Ordinarily we would have had a communications man in your place. One of our own, I mean. Since you have communications experience you will handle the wireless. No problem, I hope."

"I can't see it very well right now . . ."

"Say, there, Owens," Michaels called upward. "How about the power?"

"Right away. I'm checking a few items."

Michaels said, "I don't believe there is anything unusual about it. It is the only non-nuclear-powered object on the ship."

"I don't expect any problems."

"Good! Relax, then. It will be a few minutes yet before we can be miniaturized. The others are busy and if you don't mind, I will talk."

"Go ahead."

Michaels adjusted himself in his seat. "We all have our specific reactions to nervousness. Some light cigarettes — no smoking on board, by the way —"

"I don't smoke."

"Some drink, some bite their nails. I talk — provided, of course, I don't choke up altogether. Right now, it's a near squeak between talking and choking. You asked about Owens. Are you nervous about him?"

"Should I be?"

"I'm sure Carter expects you to be. A suspicious man, that Carter. Paranoid tendencies. I suspect that Carter has brooded over the fact that Owens was the man in the car with Benes at the time of the accident."

Grant said, "That thought has occurred even to me. But what does it mean? If you're implying that Owens might have arranged the incident, the interior of the car was a poor place to be."

"I don't suggest anything of the sort," said Michaels, shaking his head vigorously. "I'm trying to penetrate Carter's reasoning. Suppose Owens were a secret enemy agent, converted to Their side on one of his trips to scientific conferences overseas . . ."

"How dramatic," said Grant, drily. "Anyone else on board attend such conferences?"

Michaels thought a moment. "As a matter of fact, we all have. Even the girl attended a short meeting last year, one at which Duval presented a paper. But anyway, suppose it was Owens who was converted. Let us say that he was assigned the task of seeing to it that Benes was to be killed. It might be necessary for him to risk his own death. The driver of the collision car knew he was going to die; the five men at the rifles knew they would die. People don't seem to mind dying."

"And Owens may be prepared to die now rather than let us succeed? Is that why he is nervous?"

"Oh, no. What you now suggest is quite unbelievable. I can imagine, for the sake of argument, that Owens might be willing to give his life for some ideal, but not that he would be willing to sacrifice the prestige of his ship by having its first big mission fail."

"Then you think we can eliminate him and forget about the possibility of funny work at the crossroads."

Michaels laughed gently, his moon-face genial. "Of course. But I'll bet Carter has considered every one of us. And that you have, too."

Grant said, "Duval, for instance?"

"Why not? Anyone at all might be on the Other Side. Not for pay, perhaps; I am sure no one here can be bought; but out of mistaken idealism. Miniaturization, for instance, is primarily a war weapon right now and many of the people here are firmly against that aspect of it. A signed statement to that effect was sent to the president some months ago; a plea to end the miniaturization race, establish a combined program with other nations for the exploration of miniaturization for peaceful research in biology and medicine in particular."

"Who were involved in that movement?"

"A great many. Duval was one of the most vociferous and outspoken leaders. And, as a matter of fact, I signed the statement as well. I assure you the signers were sincere. I was and I am. It is possible to argue that Benes' device for unlimited duration of miniaturization, if it works, would greatly increase the danger of war and annihilation. If so, I suppose Duval or myself would be eager to see Benes dead before he can speak. For myself, I can deny that I am so motivated. To such an extreme, in any case. As for Duval, his great problem is his unpleasant personality. There are many who would be eager to suspect him of anything."

Michaels twisted in his seat and said, "And that girl there."

"She signed, too?"

"No, the statement was for senior personnel only. But why is she here?"

"Because Duval insisted. We were there when it happened."

"Yes, but why should she be available for his insisting? She is young and quite pretty. He is twenty years older than she and is not interested in her — or in any human being. Can she be eager to come along for Duval — or for some other more political reason?"

Grant said, "Are you jealous, Dr. Michaels?"

Michaels looked startled. Slowly, he smiled. "You know, I never really thought of that. I'll bet I am. I'm no older than Duval and if she is really interested in older men, it would certainly be pleasanter to have her prefer me. But even allowing for my prejudice, there's room for wondering about her motives."

Michaels' smile faded and he grew glumly serious once more. "And then, after all, the safety of this ship depends not only on ourselves but on those outside who are to a certain extent in control of us. Colonel Reid was as much in favor of the petition as any of us, although as a military officer he could not engage in political activity. Yet though his name was absent from the petition, his voice wasn't. He and Carter quarreled over that. They were good friends before."

"Too bad," said Grant.

"And Carter himself. His very paranoia. The stresses of the work here might have created instability in the sanest of men. I wonder if one can be entirely sure that Carter hasn't grown somewhat twisted . . ."

"Do you think he has?"

Michaels spread out his arms. "No, of course not. I told you. This is therapeutic talk. Would you rather I sat here and merely perspired, or that I screamed softly?"

Grant said, "No, I guess not. In fact, please go ahead. As long as I listen to you, I have no time to panic myself. It seems to me you've mentioned everyone."

"Not at all. I have deliberately left the least suspicious character for last. In fact, we might say as a general rule that the seemingly least suspicious character is bound to be guilty. Wouldn't you say so?"

"Obviously," said Grant. "And this least suspicious character is who? Or is this the place where a shot rings out and you crumple to the floor just before you name the identity of the fiend?"

"No one seems to be aiming at me," said Michaels. "I think I will have time. The least suspicious character is, obviously, you yourself, Grant. Who would be less suspicious than the trusted agent, assigned to see the ship safely through the mission? Can you really be trusted, Grant?"

"I'm not sure. You have only my word and what's that worth?"

"Exactly. You have been on the Other Side, been there oftener and under more obscure circumstances than anyone else on this ship, I'm certain. Suppose that in one way or another, you have been bought off."

"Possible, I suppose," said Grant, unemotionally, "but I brought Benes here safely."

"So you did; knowing, perhaps, that he would be taken care of at the next stage, leaving you in the clear and fit for further duties, as you are now."

Grant said, "I think you mean this."

But Michaels shook his head. "No, I don't. And I'm sorry; I think I'm beginning to grow offensive." He pinched his nose and said, "I wish they would begin miniaturizing. After that, I might have less time to think."

Grant felt embarrassed. There was a naked look of apprehension on Michaels' face as the skin of banter peeled off. He called up, "How about it, captain?"

"All set, all set," came Owens' metal-harsh voice.

The lights went on. At once, Duval pulled out several drawers at his side of the ship and began to look over the charts. Cora inspected the laser with care.

Grant said, "May I come up there, Owens?"

"You can stick your head up here if you want to," replied Owens. "There isn't room for anything more."

Grant said under his breath, "Take it easy, Dr. Michaels. I'll be gone for a few minutes and you can jitter, if you feel like, without being watched."

Michaels' voice was dry and his words seemed to grind out with difficulty. "You are a considerate man, Grant. If I had had my natural sleep . . ."

Grant rose and stepped back, grinning at Cora who stepped out of his way coolly. He then moved quickly up the ladder, looked up and about and said, "How will you know where to go?"

Owens said, "I've got Michaels' charts here." He flipped a switch and on one of the screens immediately before him was a replica of the circulatory system, the one Grant had already seen several times before. Owens touched another switch and parts of the chart glowed an iridescent yellow-orange.

"Our projected route," he said. "Michaels will be directing me when necessary, and since we are nuclear-fueled, Carter and the rest will be able to follow us with precision. They will help direct us, if you take care of your end with the wireless."

"You've got a complicated set of controls here."

"It's damned sophisticated," said Owens, with obvious pride. "A button for everything, so to speak, and as compact as I could make it. This was going to be used for deep-sea work, you know."

Grant swung down again and again Cora made way for him. She was deep in concentration over her laser, working with what were virtually watchmaker's tools.

"That looks complicated," said Grant.

Cora said briefly, "A ruby laser, if you know what that is."

"I know it puts out a tight beam of coherent monochromatic light, but I haven't the foggiest notion as to how it works."

"Then I suggest you go back to your seat and let me work."

"Yes, ma'am. But if you have any footballs you want strung, you let me know."

Cora put down a small screwdriver, brushed her rubber-gloved fingers together and said, "Mr. Grant?"

"Yes, ma'am?"

"Are you going to make this entire venture hideous with your notion of fun?"

"No, I won't, but—well, how do I talk to you?"

"Like a fellow-member of the crew."

"You're also a young woman."

"I know that, Mr. Grant, but what concern is that of yours? It's not necessary to assure me with every remark and gesture that you're aware of my sex. It's wearisome and unnecessary. After this is all over, if you still feel called upon to go through whatever rituals you are accustomed to performing before young women, I will deal with you in whatever fashion seems advisable, but for now . . ."

"All right. It's a date, for afterward."

"And Mr. Grant?"

"Yes?"

"Don't be defensive about once having been a football player. I really don't care."

Grant swallowed and said, "Something tells me my rituals are going to be tromped on, but . . ."

She was paying no attention but had returned to the laser. Grant couldn't help watching, his hand on the counter, following the minutest movement of her sure-fingered adjustments.

"Oh, if you could only frivol," he breathed, and fortunately she didn't hear him, or, at least, showed no signs of having done so.

Without warning, she placed her hand on his and Grant found himself starting slightly at the touch of her warm fingers.

She said, "Excuse me!" and moved his hand to one side, then released it. Almost at once she depressed a contact on the laser and a hair-thin streak of red light shot out, striking the metal disc over which his hand had just been resting. A tiny hole appeared at once and there was the thin odor of metal vapor. Had Grant's hand remained in place, the thin hole would have been in his thumb.

Grant said, "You might have warned me."

Cora said, "There is no reason for you to be standing here, is there?"

She lifted the laser, ignoring his offered help and turned toward the storeroom.

"Yes, miss," said Grant, humbly. "When near you henceforward I shall be careful where I place my hand."

Cora looked back as though startled and rather uncertain. Then, for a moment, she smiled.

Grant said, "Careful. The cheeks may crack."

Her smile vanished at once. "You promised," she said, icily, and moved into the workroom.

The voice of Owens came from above. "Grant! Check the wireless!"

"Right," called Grant. "I'll be seeing you, Cora. Afterward!"

He slipped back into his seat and looked at the wireless for the first time. "This seems to be a Morse code device."

Michaels looked up. Some of the grayness had left his face. "Yes, it's technically difficult to transmit voice across the miniaturization gap. I assume you can handle code."

"Of course." He beat out a rapid message. After a pause, the public address system in the miniaturization room boomed out with a sound level easily heard within the *Proteus*:

"Message received. Wish to confirm. Message reads: MISS PETERSON SMILED."

Cora, just returning to her seat, looked outraged and said, "Good grief."

Grant bent over the wireless and tapped out: CORRECT!

The return this time was in code. Grant listened, then called out, "Message received from outside: PREPARE FOR MINIATURIZATION."

CHAPTER 6 MINIATURIZATION

GRANT, not knowing how to prepare, sat where he was. Michaels rose with an almost convulsive suddenness, looking about as though making a last-minute check of all facilities.

Duval, having put his charts aside, began to fumble at his harness.

"May I help, doctor?" asked Cora.

He looked up. "Eh? Oh, no. It's just a matter of getting this buckle straight. Here we are."

"Doctor . . ."

"Yes?" He looked up again and was suddenly all concern over her apparent difficulty in expressing herself. "Is anything wrong with the laser, Miss Peterson?"

"Oh, no. It's just that I'm sorry I was the cause of unpleasantness between yourself and Dr. Reid."

"That was nothing. Don't think of it."

"And thank you for arranging to have me come."

Duval said, seriously, "It is quite necessary for me to have you. I couldn't rely on anyone else as I do on you."

Cora moved to Grant who, having turned to watch Duval, was now fiddling with his own harness.

"Do you know how to work that?" she asked.

"It seems more complicated than the ordinary aircraft seat-belt."

"Yes, it is. Here, you've got this hooked incorrectly. Allow me." She leaned across him and Grant found himself staring at one cheek at close quarters and catching the understated delicacy of light scent. He restrained himself.

Cora said in a low voice, "I'm sorry if I've been hard on you, but my position is a difficult one."

"I find it delightful at the moment — no, forgive me. That slipped out."

She said, "I have a position at the CMDF quite analogous to that of a number of men but I find myself blocked at every step by the completely extraneous fact of my sex. Either I receive too much consideration or too much condescension and I want neither. Not at work, at any rate. It leaves me a bundle of frustration."

Grant thought the obvious answer but didn't say it. It was going to be a strain if he were going to refrain continually from the obvious; more, perhaps, than he would be able to bear.

He said, "Whatever your sex, and at this point I'll be careful not to commit myself, you're the calmest person here except for Duval, and I don't think he knows he's here."

"Don't underestimate him, Mr. Grant. He knows he's here, I assure you. If he's calm, it's because he realizes that the importance of this mission is greater than that of his individual life."

"Because of Benes' secret?"

"No. Because this will be the first time miniaturization has been used on this scale; and that it is being used for the purpose of saving life."

Grant said, "Will it be safe to use that laser? After what it nearly did to my finger?"

"In Dr. Duval's hands that laser beam will destroy the clot without disturbing one molecule of the surrounding tissue."

"You have a high estimate of his ability."

"It is the world's estimate. And I share it with reason. I have been with him ever since I got my master's degree."

"I suspect he shows you neither too much condescension nor too much consideration merely because you are a woman."

"No, he doesn't."

She returned to her seat and slipped on her own harness in one fluid motion.

Owens called, "Dr. Michaels, we're waiting."

Michaels, having stepped from his seat and moved slowly about the cabin seemed, for the moment, abstracted and uncertain. Then, looking quickly from one strapped person to another said, "Oh, yes," sat down and adjusted his own harness.

Owens swung down from his bubble, checked each harness quickly, mounted again and put on his own. "Okay, Mr. Grant. Tell them we're ready."

Grant did so and the loudspeaker sounded almost at once: ATTENTION, PROTEUS. ATTENTION, PROTEUS. THIS IS THE LAST VOICE MESSAGE YOU WILL RECEIVE UNTIL MISSION IS COMPLETED. YOU HAVE SIXTY MINUTES OBJECTIVE TIME. ONCE MINIATURIZATION IS COMPLETE, THE SHIP'S TIME-RECORDER WILL GIVE THE SIXTY READING. YOU ARE AT ALL TIMES TO BE AWARE OF THAT READING WHICH WILL BE REDUCED ONE UNIT AT A TIME, EACH MINUTE. DO NOT — REPEAT, DO NOT — TRUST YOUR SUBJECTIVE FEELINGS AS TO TIME PASSAGE. YOU MUST BE OUT OF BENES' BODY BEFORE THE READING REACHES ZERO. IF YOU ARE NOT, YOU WILL KILL BENES REGARDLESS OF THE SUCCESS OF THE SURGERY. GOOD LUCK!"

The voice stopped and Grant could find nothing more original with which to encourage his sinking spirits than, "This is it!"

To his own surprise, he found he had said it aloud.

Michaels, next to him, said, "Yes, it is," and managed a weak smile.

•

In the observation tower, Carter waited. He caught himself wishing he were in the *Proteus*, rather than outside it. It would be a difficult hour and it would be easier to be in a position where he would know at each moment the events of that moment.

He quivered at the sudden, sharp tapping of the wireless message over an open circuit. The aide at the receiving end spoke quietly: "*Proteus* reports all secured."

Carter called out, "Miniaturizer!"

The proper switch, labeled MIN, at the proper panel was touched by the proper finger of the proper technician. It's like a ballet, thought Carter, with everyone in place and every motion prescribed, in a dance the end of which none could see.

The touch upon the switch was reflected in the fading to one side of the wall at the end of the miniaturizing room and the revelation, bit by bit, of a huge, honeycombed disc, suspended from a rail running along the ceiling. It moved toward and over the *Proteus*, making its way silently and without friction on air jets that kept its suspension arm a tenth of an inch above the railing.

•

To those inside the *Proteus*, the geometrically-riddled disc was clearly visible, approaching like a pockmarked monster.

Michaels' forehead and bald head were unpleasantly beaded with perspiration. "That," he said, in a muffled voice, "is the miniaturizer."

Grant opened his mouth, but Michaels added hurriedly, "Don't ask me how it works. Owens knows, but I don't."

Grant cast an involuntary glance up and back toward Owens, who seemed to be tightening and growing rigid. One of his hands was clearly visible and was grasping a bar which, Grant guessed, was one of the ship's more important units of control; grasping it as though the sensation of something material and powerful lent him comfort. Or perhaps the touch of any part of the ship he had himself designed was consoling. He, more than anyone, must know the strength — or the weakness — of the bubble that would keep them surrounded by a microscopic bit of normality.

Grant looked away and found his eye stumbling over Duval, whose thin lips were faintly stretched into a smile.

"You look uneasy, Mr. Grant. Is it not your profession to be in uneasy situations without being uneasy?"

Damn it! For how many decades had the public been fed fairy tales about undercover agents? "No, Doctor," said Grant, levelly. "In my profession to be in an uneasy situation without being uneasy is to be quickly dead. We are expected only to act intelligently, regardless of the state of our feelings. You, I take it, do not feel uneasy."

"No. I feel interested. I feel saturated with — with a sense of wonder. I am unbearably curious and excited, not uneasy."

"What are the chances of death, in your opinion?"

"Small, I hope. And in any case, I have the consolations of religion. I have confessed, and for me death is but a doorway."

Grant had no reasonable answer to that and made none. For him, death was a blank wall with but one side, but he had to admit that however logical that seemed to his mind, it offered little consolation at the moment against the worm of uneasiness that (as Duval had correctly noted) lay coiled inside that same mind.

He was miserably aware that his own forehead was wet,

perhaps as wet as Michaels', and that Cora was looking at him with what his sense of shame immediately translated into contempt.

He said, impulsively, "And have you confessed *your* sins, Miss Peterson?"

She said, coolly, "Which sins do you have in mind, Mr. Grant?"

He had no answer for that either, so he slumped in his chair and looked up at the miniaturizer, which was now exactly overhead.

"What do you feel when you are being miniaturized, Dr. Michaels?"

"Nothing, I suppose. It is a form of motion, a collapsing inward, and if it is done at a constant rate there is no more sensation in that than in moving down an escalator at constant speed."

"That's the theory, I suppose." Grant kept his eyes fixed on the miniaturizer. "What is the actual sensation?"

"I don't know. I have never experienced it. However, animals in the process of miniaturization never act in the slightest bit disturbed. They continue their normal actions without interruption, as I have personally noted."

"Animals?" Grant turned to stare at Michaels in sudden indignation. "*Animals?* Has any man ever been miniaturized?"

"I'm afraid," said Michaels, "that we have the honor of being the first."

"How thrilling. Let me ask another question. How far down has any living creature — any living creature at all — been miniaturized?"

"Fifty," said Michaels, briefly.

"What?"

"Fifty. I mean the reduction is such that the linear dimensions are one-fiftieth normal."

"Like reducing me to a height of nearly one and a half inches."

"Yes."

"But we're going far past that point."

"Yes. To nearly a million, I think. Owens can give you the exact figure."

"The exact figure does not matter. The point is it's much more intense a miniaturization than has ever been tried before."

"That is correct. This has been said earlier — or haven't you been listening?"

"Apparently not," said Grant, grimly. "Some things don't get absorbed first time around. But tell me, do you think we can bear up under all the honors we are being showered with in the way of pioneering?"

"Mr. Grant," said Michaels, and from somewhere he dredged up the touch of humor that marked his words, "I'm afraid we must. We are being miniaturized now; right now; and obviously you don't feel it."

"Good God!" muttered Grant, and looked up again with a kind of frozen and fixed attention.

The bottom of the miniaturizer was glowing with a colorless light that blazed without blinding. It did not seem to be sensed with the eyes but with the nerves generally, so that when Grant closed his eyes, all actual objects blanked out but the light was still visible as a general, featureless radiance.

Michaels must have been watching Grant close his eyes uselessly, for he said, "It's not light. It's not electromagnetic radiation of any sort. It's a form of energy that is not part of our normal universe. It affects the nerve endings and our brain interprets it as light because it knows of no other way of interpreting it."

"Is it dangerous in any way?"

"Not as far as is known, but I must admit that nothing has ever been exposed to it at this intense a level."

"Pioneering again," muttered Grant.

Duval cried out, "Glorious! Like the light of creation!"

The hexagonal tiles beneath the vessel were glowing in response to the radiation and the *Proteus* was itself ablaze both within and without. The chair in which Grant sat might have been made of fire, but it remained solid and cool. Even the air about him lit up and he breathed cold illumination.

His fellow-passengers and his own hands were frigidly aglow.

Duval's luminous hand marked out the sign of the cross in a sparking movement and his shining lips moved.

Grant said, "Are you suddenly afraid, Dr. Duval?"

Duval said softly, "One prays not only out of fear, but out of gratitude for the privilege of seeing the great wonders of God."

Grant inwardly acknowledged himself to be the loser of that exchange, too. He wasn't doing at all well.

Owens cried out, "Look at the walls."

They were drifting away in all directions at a visible rate of speed now and the ceiling was moving upward. All ends of the large room were shrouded in thick, increasing gloom, all the thicker for being seen through shining air. The miniaturizer was now an enormous thing, its limits and boundaries not quite visible. In each indentation of its honeycomb there was a fragment of the unearthly light; a regular marching of so many brilliant stars in a black sky.

Grant found himself losing his nervousness in the excitement of it. With an effort, he glanced hastily at the others. All of them were looking upward, hypnotized by the light, by the vast distances that had been created out of nowhere, by a room that had enlarged into a universe, and a universe that had grown out of ken.

Without warning, the light dimmed to a dull red and the

wireless signal sounded in staccato bursts with a sharp, echoing ring. Grant started.

Michaels said, "Belinski at Rockefeller said subjective sensations must change with miniaturization. He was largely ignored, but that signal certainly sounds different."

Grant said, "Your voice doesn't."

"That is because you and I are both equally miniaturized. I'm talking about sensations that must cross the miniaturization gap; sensations from out there."

Grant translated and read out the message that had come in: "MINIATURIZATION TEMPORARILY HALTED. IS ALL WELL? REPLY AT ONCE!"

"Is everyone all right?" Grant called out, sardonically. There was no answer and he said, "Silence gives consent," and tapped out: ALL WELL.

•

Carter licked lips that remained dry. He watched with painful concentration as the miniaturizer took on its glow and he knew that everyone in the room down to the least essential technician was doing the same.

Living human beings had never been miniaturized. Nothing as large as the *Proteus* had ever been miniaturized. Nothing, man or animal, living or dead, large or small, had ever been miniaturized so drastically. The responsibility was his. All responsibility in this continuing nightmare was his.

"There she goes!" came an almost exultant whisper from the technician at the miniaturization button. The phrase came clearly over the communications system, as Carter watched the *Proteus* shrink.

It did so slowly at first, so that one could only tell it was happening by the change in the way it overlapped the hexagonal structures that made up the floor. Those that were partially revealed beyond the edge of the ship's structure crept outward, and eventually tiles that had earlier been completely hidden began to show. All around the *Proteus* the hexagonals emerged, and the rate of miniaturization accelerated until the ship was shrinking like a patch of ice on a warm surface.

Carter had watched miniaturization a hundred times, but never with quite the effect upon himself that he was experiencing now. It was as though the ship were hurtling down a long, infinitely long hole; falling in absolute silence and growing smaller and smaller as the distance increased to miles, to tens of miles, to hundreds. The ship was a white beetle now, resting upon the central hexagon immediately under the miniaturizer; resting upon the one red hexagon in the world of white ones, the Zero Module. The *Proteus* was still falling, still shrinking, and Carter, with an effort, raised his hand. The glow of the miniaturizer faded to a dull red and miniaturization stopped.

"Find out how they are before we continue."

They might conceivably be dead or, just as bad, unable to perform their tasks with reasonable efficiency. In that case, they had lost and it would be well to know now.

The communications technician said, "Answer returned and reads: ALL WELL."

Carter thought: If they're unable to operate, they might be unable to realize they're unable. But there would be no way to check that. One had to pretend all was well if the crew of the *Proteus* said all was well.

Carter said, "Elevate the ship."

CHAPTER 7 SUBMERGENCE

SLOWLY, the Zero Module began to lift from the floor, a smooth hexagonal pillar, with red top and white sides, bearing the inch-wide *Proteus* upon itself. When the top was four feet off the floor it stopped.

"Ready for phase two, sir," came the voice of one of the technicians.

Carter looked briefly at Reid, who nodded.

"Phase two," said Carter.

A panel slid open and a handling device (a gigantic waldo, so named by the early nuclear technicians from a character in a science fiction story of the 1940s, Carter had once been told) moved in on silent air jets. It was fourteen feet high and consisted of pulleys on a tripod, pulleys which controlled a vertical arm, dangling down from a horizontal extensor. The arm itself was in stages, each shorter and on a smaller scale than the one above. In this case, there were three stages and the lowest one, two inches long, was fitted with steel wires a quarter-inch thick, curved to meet each other in interlocking fashion.

The base of the device carried the CMDF insigne and below it was the inscription MIN PRECISION HANDLING.

Three technicians had entered with the handling device and behind them a uniformed nurse waited with visible impatience. The brown hair under her nurse's cap looked hastily adjusted as though on that one day she had other things on her mind.

Two of the technicians adjusted the arm of the waldo directly over the shrunken *Proteus*. For the fine adjustment, three hair-thin beams of light reached from the arm support to the surface of the Zero Module. The distance of each beam from the center of the Module was translated into light intensity upon a small circular screen divided into three segments, meeting in its center.

The light intensities, clearly unequal, shifted delicately as the third technician adjusted a knob. With the skill of practice, he brought the three segments to equal intensity in a matter of seconds, equal enough to wipe out the boundaries between them. The technician then threw a switch and locked the waldo into position. The centering lines of light flicked off and the broader beam of a searchlight illuminated the *Proteus* by indirect reflection.

Another control was manipulated, and the arm sank toward the *Proteus*. Slowly and gently it came down, the technician holding his breath. He had probably handled more miniaturized objects than anyone in the country, possibly more than anyone in the world (although no one knew all the details of what was going on over There, of course), but this was something unprecedented.

He was going to lift something with a greater normal-mass by many times than he had ever done before, and what he was going to lift contained five living human beings. Even a small, barely visible tremor might be enough to kill.

The prongs below opened and slowly slipped down over

the *Proteus.* The technician stopped them and tried to have his eyes assure himself that what his instruments told him was true. The prongs were accurately centered. Slowly, they closed, bit by bit, until they met underneath the ship and formed a close-knit, precision-adjusted cradle. The Zero Module then dropped and left the *Proteus* suspended in the cradle claws.

The Zero Module did not stop at floor level, but sank below. Underneath the suspended ship was, for a few minutes, nothing but a hole. Then, sheer glass walls began to rise upward from within the gap left by the Zero Module. When those walls, clear and cylindrical, had emerged a foot and a half, the meniscus of a clear liquid showed. When the Zero Module had emerged to floor level again, what was resting upon it was a cylinder, one foot wide and four feet tall, two-thirds filled with fluid. The cylinder rested on a circling cork base on which the lettering read, *Saline Solution.*

The arm of the waldo, which had not budged during this change, was now suspended over the solution. The ship was held within the upper portion of the cylinder, a foot above the solution level.

The arm was dropping now, slowly and more slowly. It stopped when the *Proteus* was almost at solution level, and then began moving with a velocity scaled down by a factor of ten thousand. The gears under the technician's immediate control moved rapidly while the ship lowered at a rate invisible to the eye.

Contact! The ship lowered further and further till it was half-submerged. The technician held it so for a moment, and then, as slowly as ever, he disengaged the claws and, making sure the individual wires would clear the ship, lifted them free of the solution.

With a subdued "Yahoo," he ran up the arm and unclamped the waldo. "Okay, let's get it out of here," he said to the two on either side and then, remembering, barked out in altered, official tones, "Ship in ampule, sir!"

Carter said, "Good! Check on the crew!"

*

The transfer from Module to ampule had been dainty enough from the standpoint of the normal world, but had been anything but from within the *Proteus.*

Grant had radioed back the ALL WELL signal and then, overcoming the initial moment of nausea at the sudden lurch upward as the Zero Module began to rise, said, "What now? More miniaturization? Anyone know?"

Owens said, "We'll have to submerge before the next stage of miniaturization."

"Submerge where?" But Grant received no answer to that. He looked out again into the dim universe of the miniaturization room and caught his first glimpse of the giants.

They were men, moving toward them, towers of men in the dim outer light, men foreshortened downward, foreshortened upward, as though viewed in giant distorting mirrors. A belt buckle was a square of metal, a foot either way. A shoe, far below, might have been a railroad car. A head far above seemed a mountainous nose surrounding the twin tunnels of the nostrils. The giants moved with odd slowness.

"Time-sense," muttered Michaels. He was squinting upward and then looking at his watch.

"What?" asked Grant.

"Another one of Belinski's suggestions; that the time sense alters with miniaturization. Ordinary time seems to lengthen and stretch so that right now, five minutes seems to last, I should judge, ten minutes. The effect grows more intense with extent of miniaturization but exactly what the relationship is, I can't say. Belinski needed the kind of experimental data we can now give him." He held out his wrist watch. "See?"

Grant looked at it, then at his own. The sweep second hand did seem to be crawling at that. He held the watch to his ear. There was only the faint whir of its tiny motor, but the tone of that whir seemed to have deepened.

"This is good," said Michaels. "We have an hour, but it may seem like several hours to us. A good number, perhaps."

"Do you mean we will move more quickly?"

"To ourselves we will move normally; but to an observer in the outer world, I suspect we will seem to be moving quickly, to be squeezing more activity into a given time. Which would, of course, be good, considering the limited time we have."

"But . . ."

Michaels shook his head, "Please! I can't explain better than that. Belinski's biophysics I think I understand, but his mathematics is beyond me. Maybe Owens can tell you."

Grant said, "I'll ask him afterward — if there is an afterward."

The ship was suddenly in the light again, ordinary white light. Motion caught Grant's eyes and he looked up. Something was descending, a giant pair of prongs moved down on either side of the ship.

Owens called out. "Everyone check their body harness."

Grant did not bother. He felt a yank behind him and he twisted around as far as the harness would allow.

Cora said, "I was checking to see if you were being tightly held."

"Only by the harness," said Grant, "but thanks."

"You're welcome." Then, turning to her right, she said, solicitously, "Dr. Duval. Your harness."

"All right. Yours."

Cora had loosened the harness so that she might reach Grant. She tightened it now and barely in time. The prongs had moved below eye-level now and were coming together like a gigantic, crushing jaw. Grant automatically stiffened. They halted, moved again, and made contact. The *Proteus* jogged and jarred and all aboard were thrown violently to the right and then, less violently, to the left. A harsh, reverberating clang filled the ship.

There was then silence and the clear sensation of suspension over emptiness. The ship swayed gently and trembled even more gently. Grant looked down and saw a vast, red surface sinking and growing dim and dark — and vanishing. He had no way of knowing what the distance to the floor was, on their present size-scale, but the sensation was like that he would have had if he had leaned out a window on the twentieth floor of an apartment building.

Something as small as the ship now was, falling that distance, ought not sustain serious damage. Air resistance would slow them to safe velocities — at least, if their smallness were all there were to it. But Grant had a lively remembrance of the point made by Owens during briefing. He himself was at this moment made up of as many atoms as a full-sized man and not as few as an object *actually* his present size would be. He was correspondingly more fragile and so was the ship. A fall from this height would smash the ship and kill the crew.

He looked at the cradle holding the ship. What they seemed to a normal man, Grant did not stop to consider. To himself they were curved, steel pillars ten feet in diameter, meshed neatly into a continuous cradle of metal. For the moment, he felt safe.

Owens called out in a voice that cracked with excitement, "Here it comes."

Grant looked quickly in various directions before making out what "it" was.

The light was glinting off the smooth, transparent surfaces of a circle of glass big enough to surround a house. It rose smoothly and rapidly; and far below — directly below — was the sudden, iridescent and twinkling reflection of lights upon water.

The *Proteus* was suspended over a lake. The glass walls of the cylinder were rising on all sides of the ship now and the surface of the lake did not appear to be more than fifty feet below them.

Grant leaned back in his chair. He had no trouble guessing what came next. He was prepared, therefore, and felt no nausea whatever when his seat seemed to drop from under him. The sensation was very much like that he had once experienced in the course of a power dive over the ocean. The plane that had engaged in that maneuver had pulled out, as it was meant to, but the *Proteus*, suddenly an air-borne submarine, was not going to.

Grant tensed his muscles, then tried to relax them in order to let the harness rather than his bones take the blow. They hit, and the shock nearly jarred his teeth from their sockets.

What Grant expected to see through the window was a spray, a wall of water shooting high. What he saw instead was a large, thick swell, smoothly rounded, speeding oilily away. Then, as they continued to sink, another and another.

The claws of the cradle unhooked and the ship jounced madly and came to a floating stop, slowly turning.

Grant let out a long breath. They were on the surface of a lake, yes, but it was like no surface he had ever seen.

Michaels said, "You expected waves, Mr. Grant?"

"Yes, I did."

"I must confess I rather did myself. The human mind, Grant, is a funny thing. It expects always to see what it had seen in the past. We are miniaturized and are put in a small container of water. It seems like a lake to us so we expect waves, foam, breakers, who knows what else. But whatever this lake appears to us to be, it is not a lake but merely a small container of water, and it has ripples and not waves. And no matter how you enlarge a ripple, it never looks like a wave!"

"Interesting enough, though," said Grant. The thick rolls of fluid, which on an ordinary scale would have made tiny ripples, continued to race outward. Reflected from the distant wall, they returned and made interference patterns that broke the rolls into separate hills, while the *Proteus* rose and fell in drastic rhythms.

"Interesting?" said Cora, indignantly. "Is that all you can say? It's simply magnificent."

"His handiwork," added Duval, "is majestic on every scale of magnitude."

"All right," said Grant, "I'll buy that. Magnificent and majestic. Check. Only a little nauseating, too, you know."

"Oh, Mr. Grant," said Cora. "You have a knack for deflating everything."

"Sorry," said Grant.

The wireless sounded and Grant sent back the ALL WELL signal again. He resisted the impulse to send back "All seasick."

Still, even Cora was beginning to look uncomfortable. Perhaps he shouldn't have put the thought into her mind.

Owens said, "We'll have to submerge manually. Grant, slip out of your harness and open valves one and two."

Grant rose unsteadily to his feet, delighted at the feeling of even the limited freedom of walking, and moved to a butterfly valve on the bulkhead, marked ONE.

"I'll take the other," said Duval. Their eyes met for a moment, and Duval, as though embarrassed by the sudden intimate awareness of another human being, smiled hesitantly. Grant smiled back and thought indignantly: Now how can she get sentimental over this mass of unawareness?

With the valves open, the surrounding fluid flowed into the

appropriate chambers of the ship, and the liquid rose all about again, higher and higher.

Grant moved part way up the ladder to the upper bubble and said, "How does it look, Captain Owens?"

Owens shook his head. "It's hard to say. The readings on the dials lack significance. They were designed with a real ocean in view. Damn it, I never designed the *Proteus* for *this.*"

"My mother never designed me for this, either, if it comes to that," said Grant. They were completely submerged now. Duval had closed both valves and Grant returned to his seat.

He put on his harness once again with an almost luxurious feeling. Once beneath the surface the erratic rise and fall of the tiny swell was gone, and there was a blessed motionlessness.

*

Carter tried to unclench his fists. So far, it had gone well. The ALL WELL had sounded from within the ship, which was now a small capsule glimmering inside the saline solution.

"Phase three," he said.

The miniaturizer, the brilliance of which had remained subdued through all the second phase, lifted into white glory again, but only from the centermost sections of the honeycomb.

Carter watched earnestly. It was hard to tell at first if what he saw were objectively real, or the straining of his mind. No, it really was shrinking again.

The inch-wide beetle was reducing in size and so, presumably, was the water in its immediate vicinity. The focus of the miniaturizing beam was tight and accurate and Carter expelled another held breath. At each stage, there was a danger peculiar to itself.

Glancingly, Carter imagined what might happen if the beam had been slightly less accurate, if half the *Proteus* had miniaturized rapidly, while the other half, caught at the boundary of the beam, had miniaturized slowly or not at all. But it hadn't happened and he strove to put it out of his mind.

The *Proteus* was a shrinking dot now, smaller, smaller, down to the barest edge of sight. Now the entire miniaturizer sprang into brilliance. It wouldn't do to try to focus the beam on something too small to see.

Right, right, thought Carter. Do the whole thing now.

The entire cylinder of liquid was now shrinking, more and more quickly, until finally it was a mere ampule, two inches high and half an inch thick, with somewhere in the miniaturized fluid an infra-miniaturized *Proteus*, no larger than the size of a large bacterium. The miniaturizer dimmed again.

"Get them," said Carter, shakily. "Get some word from them."

He breathed through a tightened throat until the ALL WELL was once more announced. Four men and a woman who, not many minutes before, had stood before him in full size and life, were tiny bits of matter within a germ-sized ship — and were still alive.

He put out his hands, palms downward. "Take out the miniaturizer on the double."

The last dim light of the miniaturizer flicked out as it moved rapidly away.

A blank, circular dial on the wall above Carter's head now flashed into a dark 60.

Carter nodded to Reid. "Take over, Don. We've got sixty minutes from this instant."

CHAPTER 8 ENTRY

THE LIGHT of the miniaturizer had flashed on again after submergence and the fluid all about had turned into a glimmering, opaque milk, but nothing followed that could be observed from within the *Proteus*. If the opacity were spreading out and the ship shrinking further, there was no way of telling.

Grant did not speak in that interval of time, nor did anyone else. It seemed to last forever. And then the light of the miniaturizer went out and Owens cried out, "Is everyone all right?"

Duval said, "I'm fine." Cora nodded. Grant lifted a reassuring hand. Michaels shrugged slightly and said, "I'm all right."

"Good! I think we're at full miniaturization now," said Owens.

He flipped a switch which hitherto he had not touched. For an anxious moment, he waited for a dial to come to life. It did, with a dark and sharp 60 limned upon it. A similar dial, lower in the ship, was visible to the other four.

The wireless rattled harshly and Grant sent back the ALL

WELL. For a moment, it was as though some climax had been reached.

Grant said, "They say outside we're at full miniaturization. You guessed correctly, Captain Owens."

"And here we are," said Owens, sighing audibly.

Grant thought: Miniaturization is complete but the mission isn't. It's just beginning. Sixty. Sixty minutes.

Aloud, he said, "Captain Owens, why is the ship vibrating? Is there anything wrong?"

Michaels said, "I feel it. It's an uneven vibration."

"I feel it, too," said Cora.

Owens came down from the bubble, mopping his forehead with a large handkerchief.

"We can't help this. It's Brownian motion."

Michaels raised his hands with an "Oh, lord," of helpless and resigned understanding.

Grant said, "Whose motion?"

"Brown's, if you must know. Robert Brown, an eighteenth century Scottish botanist, who first observed it. You see, we're being bombarded by water molecules from all sides. If we were full size, the molecules would be so tiny in comparison that their collisions wouldn't affect us. However, the fact that we're tremendously miniaturized brings about the same results that would follow if we had remained constant and everything in our surroundings had been greatly magnified."

"Like the water all around."

"Exactly. So far, we're not badly off. The water around us has been partly miniaturized with us. When we get into the blood stream, though, each water molecule, on our present scale, will weigh a milligram or so. They will still be too small to affect us individually, but thousands will be striking us simultaneously from all directions, and those strikes won't be distributed evenly. Several hundred more might strike from the right than from the left at any given instant, and the combined force of those several hundred extra will shove us toward the left. The next instant we may be forced a bit downward and so on. This vibration we feel now is the result of such random molecular strikes. It will be worse later on."

"Fine," groaned Grant. "Nausea, here I come."

"It will only be for an hour at most," said Cora, angrily. "I wish you would act more grown up."

Michaels said, with obvious worry, "Can the ship take the battering, Owens?"

Owens said, "I think so. I tried to make some calculations concerning it in advance. From what I feel now, I think my estimates weren't far off. This can be endured."

Cora said, "Even if the ship is battered and crushed, it's bound to stand up under the bombardment for a little while. If everything goes well, we can get to the clot and take care of it in fifteen minutes or less and after that it really doesn't matter."

Michaels brought his fist down on the arm-rest of his chair. "Miss Peterson, you are speaking nonsense. What do you suppose would happen, if we managed to reach the clot, destroy it, restore Benes to health and then have the *Proteus* smashed to rubble immediately afterward? I mean aside from our deaths, which, for the sake of further argument, I am ready to consider nothing? It would mean Benes' death, too."

"We understand that," broke in Duval, stiffly.

"Your assistant apparently does not. If this ship were to be beaten into fragments, Miss Peterson, then when the sixty minutes — no, fifty-nine — are up, each individual fragment, however small, would enlarge to normal size. Even if the ship were dissolved into atoms, each atom would enlarge and Benes would be permeated through and through with the matter of ourselves and the ship."

Michaels took a deep breath, one that sounded almost like a snort. He went on, "It is easy to get us out of Benes' body if we are intact. If the ship is in fragments, there will be no way of flushing every fragment out of Benes' body. No matter what is done, enough will remain to kill him at deminiaturization time. Do you understand?"

Cora seemed to shrink within herself. "I hadn't thought of that."

"Well, think of it," said Michaels. "You, too, Owens. Now I want to know again, will the *Proteus* stand up under the Brownian motion? I don't mean only till we reach the clot. I mean till we reach it, finish it, and *return!* Consider what you say, Owens. If you don't think the ship can survive then we have no right to go on."

"Well, then," interposed Grant, "stop hectoring, Dr. Michaels, and give Captain Owens a chance to talk."

Owens said doggedly, "I came to no final opinion till I felt the partial Brownian motion we now experience. It is my feeling at the present moment that we can stand up to sixty full minutes of the full pounding."

"The question is: Ought we to take the risk on the mere strength of Captain Owens' feelings?"

"Not at all," said Grant, "the question is: Will I accept Captain Owens' estimate of the situation? Please remember that General Carter said I was to make the policy decisions. I am accepting Owens' statement simply because we have no one of greater authority or with a better understanding of the ship to consult."

"Well, then," said Michaels, "what is your decision?"

"I accept Owens' estimate. We proceed with the mission."

Duval said, "I agree with you, Grant."

Michaels, slightly flushed, nodded his head. "All right, Grant. I was merely making what seemed to me a legitimate point." He took his seat.

Grant said, "It was a most legitimate point, and I'm glad you raised it." He remained standing, by the window.

Cora joined him after a moment and said, quietly, "You didn't sound frightened, Grant."

Grant smiled joylessly. "Ah, but that's because I'm a good actor, Cora. If it were anyone else taking the responsibility for the decision, I would have made a terrific speech in favor of quitting. You see, I have cowardly feelings, but I try not to make cowardly decisions."

Cora watched him for a moment. "I get the notion, Mr. Grant, that you have to work awfully hard, sometimes, to make yourself sound worse than you really are."

"Oh, I don't know. I have a talent . . ."

At that point the *Proteus* moved convulsively, first to one side, then to the other, in great sweeps.

Lord, thought Grant, we're sloshing.

He caught Cora's elbow, and forced her toward her seat. Then, with difficulty, he took his own, while Owens swayed and stumbled in an attempt to make it up the ladder, crying out, "Damn it, they might have warned us."

Grant braced himself against his chair and noted the time-recorder reading to be 59. A long minute, he thought. Michaels had said the time-sense slowed with miniaturization and he was obviously right. There would be more time for thought and action.

More time for second thought and panic, too.

The *Proteus* moved even more abruptly. Would the ship break up before the mission proper had even started?

*

Reid took Carter's place at the window. The ampule, with its few milliliters of partially miniaturized water, in which the completely miniaturized and quite invisible *Proteus* was submerged, gleamed on the Zero Module, like some rare gem on a velvet cushion.

At least Reid thought the metaphor, but did not allow it to console him. Calculations had been precise and the miniaturization technique could produce sizes that would fully match the precision of the calculation. That calculation, however, had been worked out in the space of a few hurried and pressure-filled hours, by means of a system of computer programming that had not been checked out.

To be sure, if the size were slightly off, it could be corrected, but the time required to do so would have to come out of the sixty minutes — and it was going to be fifty-nine in fifteen seconds.

"Phase four," he said.

The waldo had already moved above the ampule, the claw adjusted for horizontal holding, rather than vertical. Again the device was centered, again the arm dropped and the claws came together with infinite delicacy.

The ampule was held with the firm gentleness of a lioness' paw upon her unruly cub.

It was the nurse's turn at last. She stepped forward briskly, took a small case from her pocket and opened it. She removed a small glass rod, holding it gingerly by a flat head set upon a slightly constricted neck. She placed it vertically over the ampule and let it slide a small fraction of an inch into it, until air pressure held it steady. She spun it gently and said, "Plunger fits."

(From his upper view, Reid smiled in tight relief, and Carter nodded his approval.)

The nurse waited and the waldo lifted its arm slowly. Smoothly, smoothly, the ampule and plunger rose. Three inches above the Zero Module, it stopped.

As gently as she might, the nurse eased the cork base off the bottom of the ampule, revealing a small nipple centered on the otherwise flat lower surface. The tiny opening in the middle of the nipple was masked with a thin plastic sheet that would not stand up against even moderate pressure, but would hold firm against leakage as long as undisturbed.

Moving quickly again, the nurse removed a stainless steel needle from the case and adjusted it over the nipple.

"Needle fits," she said.

What had been an ampule had become a hypodermic needle.

A second set of claws swung out from the waldo and was adjusted to the head of the plunger, then clamped into place. The entire waldo, carrying the hypodermic needle in its two claws now moved smoothly toward the large double doors that opened at its approach.

No human being could, with his unaided eyes, have detected any motion in the liquid so steadily transported by the inhumanly smooth movement of the machine. Both Carter and Reid, however, understood quite well that even microscopic motion would be nothing less than storm-tossing to the crew of the *Proteus*.

When the device entered the operating room and stopped at the table, Carter recognized this fact by ordering: "Contact the *Proteus!*"

The reply was ALL WELL BUT A LITTLE SHOOK, and Carter forced a grin at that.

Benes was lying on the operating table, a second focus of interest in the room. The thermal blanket covered him to the collarbone. Thin rubber tubes led from the blanket to the central thermal unit under the operating table.

Forming a rough semi-sphere beyond Benes' shaven, grid-marked head were a group of sensitive detectors intended to react to the presence of radioactive emissions.

A team of gauze-masked surgeons and their assistants hovered about Benes, their eyes fixed solemnly on the approaching device. The time-recorder was prominent on one wall and at this point it changed from 59 to 58.

The waldo stopped at bedside.

Two of the sensors moved from their place, as though they were suddenly endowed with life. Following the long-distance manipulations of a quick-working technician, they lined up on either side of the hypodermic, one adjacent to the ampule and one to the needle.

A small screen on the technician's desk woke to greenish life as a blip appeared upon it, faded, was reinforced, faded again, and so on.

The technician said, "*Proteus* radioactivity being received."

Carter brought his hands together in a harsh clap and reacted with grim satisfaction. Another hurdle, one which he had not been allowing himself to face, had been overcome. It was not merely radioactivity that had to be sensed, but radioactive particles that had themselves been miniaturized, and that, because of their incredibly tiny, infra-atomic size, could pass through any ordinary sensor without affecting it. The particles had, therefore, to pass through a deminiaturizer first, and the necessary juxtaposition of deminiaturizer and sensor had only been improvised in the frantic hours of the early morning.

The waldo, holding the plunger of the hypodermic, now pushed downward with a smoothly increasing pressure. The fragile plastic barrier between ampule and needle broke and, after a moment, a tiny bubble began to appear at the tip of the needle. It dropped off into a small container placed underneath; a second bubble and a third followed.

The plunger sank, and so did the water level within the ampule. And then, the blip on the screen before the technician's eyes changed position.

"*Proteus* in needle," he called out.

The plunger held.

Carter looked at Reid, "Okay?"

Reid nodded. He said, "We can insert now."

The hypodermic needle was tilted into a sharp slant by the

two sets of claws and the waldo began to move again, this time toward a spot on Benes' neck which a nurse now hastily swabbed with alcohol. A small circle was marked on the neck, within the circle a smaller cross, and toward the center of the cross the tip of the hypodermic needle approached. The sensors followed it.

A moment of hesitation as the needle-tip touched the neck. It punctured and entered a prescribed distance, the plunger moved slightly, and the sensor-technician called out, "*Proteus* injected."

The waldo moved off hurriedly. The cloud of sensors moved in, like eagerly reaching antennae, settling down all over Benes' head and neck.

"Tracking," called out the sensor-technician, and flipped a switch. A half-dozen screens, each with its blip in a different position, lit up. Somewhere the information on those screens was fed into a computer which controlled the huge map of Benes' circulatory system. On that map, a bright dot sprang into life in the carotid artery. Into that artery, the *Proteus* had been injected.

Carter considered praying but didn't know how. On the map there seemed only the smallest distance between the position of the dot of light and the position of the blood clot on the brain.

Carter watched as the time-recorder moved to 57, then followed the unmistakable and rather rapid motion of the dot of light along the artery, headward and toward the clot.

Momentarily, he closed his eyes and thought: Please. If there is anything out there somewhere, *please.*

*

Grant called out, having a little difficulty catching his breath, "We've been moved toward Benes. They say they're getting us into the needle and then into his neck. And I've told them we're a little shook. Whoof — a little shook!"

"Good," said Owens. He battled with the controls, trying to guess at the rocking motions and neutralize their effect. He wasn't very successful.

Grant said, "Listen, why — why do we have to get into the — oof — needle?"

"We'll be more constricted there. Moving the needle will hardly affect us then. Another — uh — thing, we want as little of the miniaturized water pumped into Benes as possible."

Cora said, "Oh, dear."

Her hair had fallen into disarray and as she tried, futilely, to move it back and out of her eyes, she nearly fell over. Grant tried to catch her but Duval had her upper arm in a firm grip.

As suddenly as the erratic rocking had started, it ceased.

"We're in the needle," said Owens with relief. He turned on the ship's outer lights.

Grant peered ahead. There was little to see. The saline solution ahead seemed to sparkle like a dusting of dim fireflies. Far up above and far down below was the distant curve of something which shone more brightly. The walls of the needle?

A quick sense of worry nagged at him. He turned to Michaels. "Doctor . . ."

Michaels' eyes were closed. They opened reluctantly and his head turned in the direction of the voice. "Yes, Mr. Grant."

"What do you see?"

Michaels stared forward, spread his hands slightly, and said, "Sparkles."

"Do you make out anything clearly? Does everything seem to dance about?"

"Yes, it does. It dances."

"Does that mean our eyes are affected by the miniaturization?"

"No, no, Mr. Grant." Michaels sighed wearily. "If you're

worried about blindness, forget it. Look around you here in the *Proteus*. Look at me. Is there anything wrong with how it looks in here?"

"No."

"Very well. In here, you are seeing miniaturized light waves with an equally miniaturized retina and all is well. But when miniaturized light waves go out there into a less miniaturized or completely unminiaturized world, they are not easily reflected. They're quite penetrating, in fact. We see only intermittent reflections here and there. Therefore, everything out there seems to flicker to us."

"I see. Thank you, Doc," said Grant.

Michaels sighed again. "I trust I get my sea legs soon. The flickering light and the Brownian motion together are giving me a headache."

"Here we go!" cried Owens, suddenly.

They were sliding forward now. The sensation was unmistakeable. The far-off, curving walls of the hypodermic needle seemed more solid now as the spotty reflection of miniaturized light from their walls blurred and melted together. It was like riding a roller coaster down an infinite incline.

Up ahead, the solidity seemed to come to an end in a tiny circle of flicker. The circle enlarged slowly, then more rapidly, then yawned into an incredible abyss—and all was flicker.

Owens said, "We're in the carotid artery now."

The time-recorder read 56.

CHAPTER 9 ARTERY

DUVAL LOOKED ABOUT with exultation. "Conceive it," he said. "Inside a human body; inside an artery. Owens! Put out the interior lights, man! Let us see God's handiwork."

The interior lights went off, but a form of ghostly light streamed in from outside, the spotty reflection of the ship's miniaturized light beams fore and aft.

Owens had brought the *Proteus* into virtual motionlessness with reference to the arterial blood stream, allowing it to sweep along with the heart-driven flow. He said, "You can remove harnesses, I think."

Duval was out of his in a bound, and Cora was with him at once. They flung themselves at the window in a kind of marveling ecstasy. Michaels rose more deliberately, threw a glance at the other two, then turned to his chart, studying it closely.

He said tightly, "Excellent precision."

"Did you think we might have missed the artery?" asked Grant.

For a moment, Michaels stared absently at Grant. Then:

"—uh—no! That would have been unlikely. But we might have penetrated past a key branch point, been unable to buck the arterial current, and lost time having to plot an alternate and poorer route. As it is, the ship is just where it ought to be." His voice quavered.

Grant said, encouragingly, "We seem to be doing well so far."

"Yes." A pause, then hastily, "From this spot, we combine ease of insertion, rapidity of current, and directness of route, so that we should reach our destination with an absolute minimum of delay."

"Well, good." Grant nodded, and turned to the window. Almost at once he was lost in amazement at the wonder of it all.

The distant wall seemed half a mile away and glowed a brilliant amber in fits and sparks, for it was mostly hidden by the vast melange of objects that floated by near the ship.

It was a vast, exotic aquarium they faced, one in which not fish but far stranger objects filled the vision. Large rubber tires, the centers depressed but not pierced through, were the most numerous objects. Each was about twice the diameter of the ship, each an orange-straw color, each sparkling and blazing intermittently, as though faceted with slivers of diamonds.

Duval said, "The color is not quite true. If it were possible to deminiaturize the light waves as they leave the ship and miniaturize the returning reflection, we would be far better off. It is important to obtain an accurate reflection."

Owens said, "You're quite right, doctor, and the work done by Johnson and Antoniani indicates that this might actually be possible. Unfortunately, the technique is not yet practical and even if it were, we couldn't have adapted the ship for the purpose in a single night."

"I suppose not," said Duval.

"But even if it's not an accurate reflection," said Cora in an awed tone, "surely it has a beauty all its own. They're like soft, squashed balloons that have trapped a million stars apiece."

"Actually, they're red blood corpuscles," said Michaels to Grant. "Red in the mass, but straw-colored individually. Those you see are fresh from the heart, carrying their load of oxygen to the head and, particularly, the brain."

Grant continued to stare about in wonder. In addition to the corpuscles, there were smaller objects; flattened plate-like affairs were rather common, for instance. (Platelets, thought Grant, as the shapes of the objects brought up brightening memories of physiology courses in college.)

One of the platelets moved gently against the ship, so closely that Grant almost had the impulse to reach out and seize it. It flattened slowly, remained in contact for a moment, then moved away, leaving particles of itself clinging to the window — a smear that slowly washed away.

"It didn't break," said Grant.

"No," said Michaels. "Had it broken, a small clot might have formed about it. Not enough to do any damage, I hope. If we were larger, though, we might run into trouble. See that!"

Grant looked off in the direction of the pointing finger. He saw small, rodlike objects, pushing fragments and detritus and, above all, red corpuscles, red corpuscles, red corpuscles. Then he made out the object at which Michaels was pointing.

It was huge, milky, and pulsating. It was granular and inside its milkiness there were black twinkles, flashing bits of black so intense as to glow with a blinding non-light of its own.

Within the mass was a darker area, dim through the surrounding milkiness, and maintaining a steady, unwinking shape. The outlines of the whole could not be clearly made out, but a milky bay suddenly extended in toward the artery wall and the mass seemed to flow into it. It faded out now, obscured by the closer objects, lost in the swirl.

"What the hell was that?" asked Grant.

"A white blood cell, of course. There aren't many of those;

at least, not compared to the red corpuscles. There are about six hundred fifty reds for every white. The whites are much bigger, though, and they can move independently. Some of them can even work their way out of the blood vessels altogether. They're frightening objects, seen on this scale of size. That's about as close as I want to be to one."

"They're the body's scavengers, aren't they?"

"Yes. We're bacterial-sized but we have a metal skin and not a mucopolysaccharide cell wall. I trust the white cells can tell the difference and that as long as we do no damage to the surrounding tissues, they won't react to us."

Grant tried to withdraw his too-particular attention from individual objects and attempted to absorb the panorama as a whole. He stepped back and narrowed his eyes.

It was a dance! Each object quivered in its position. The smaller the object, the more pronounced the quiver. It was like a colossal and unruly ballet in which the choreographer had gone mad and the dancers were caught in the grip of an eternally insane dance.

Grant closed his eyes. "Feel it? The Brownian motion, I mean."

Owens answered, "Yes, I feel it. It's not as bad as I thought it would be. The blood stream is viscous, much more viscous than the saline solution we were in, and the high viscosity damps out the motion."

Grant felt the ship move under his feet, first this way, then that, but only soggily, not sharply as had been true while they were still in the hypodermic. The protein content of the fluid portion of the blood, the "plasma proteins" (the phrase came swimming to Grant out of the past) cushioned the ship.

Not bad at all. He felt cheered. Perhaps all would be well yet.

Owens said, "I suggest you all return to your seats now.

We will be approaching a branch in the artery soon and I am going to move over to one side."

The others settled themselves into their seats, still watching their surroundings in absorption.

"I think it's a shame that we'll only have a few minutes for this," said Cora. "Dr. Duval, what are those?"

A mass of very tiny structures, clinging together and forming a tight spiral-shaped pipe, passed by. Several more followed, each expanding and contracting as it went.

"Ah," said Duval, "I don't recognize *that.*"

"A virus, perhaps," suggested Cora.

"A little too large for virus, I think, and certainly like none I've seen. Owens, are we equipped to take samples?"

Owens said, "We can get out of the ship, if we have to, Doctor, but we can't stop for samples."

"Come now, we may not have this chance again." Duval rose testily to his feet. "Let's get a piece of that into the ship. Miss Peterson, you . . ."

Owens said, "This ship has a mission, Doctor."

"It doesn't matter to . . ." began Duval, but then broke off at the firm grip of Grant's hand on his shoulder.

"If you don't mind, Doctor," said Grant, "let's not argue about this. We have a job to do and we won't stop to pick up anything or turn aside to pick up anything or as much as slow down to pick up anything. I take it you understand that and will not raise the subject again."

In the uncertain, flickering light reflected from the arterial world outside, Duval was clearly frowning.

"Oh, well," he said, ungraciously, "they've gotten away anyhow."

Cora said, "Once we complete this job, Dr. Duval, there will be methods developed for miniaturization for indefinite intervals. We can then take part in a real exploration."

"Yes, I suppose you're right."

Owens said, "Arterial wall to the right."

The *Proteus* had made a long, sweeping curve and the wall seemed about a hundred feet away, now. The somewhat corrugated amber stretch of endothelial layer that made up the inner lining of the artery was clearly visible in all its detail.

"Hah," said Duval, "what a way to check on atherosclerosis. You can count the plaques."

"You could peel them off, too, couldn't you?" asked Grant.

"Of course. Consider the future. A ship can be sent through a clogged arterial system, loosening and detaching the sclerotic regions, breaking them up, boring and reaming out the tubes. Pretty expensive treatment, however."

"Maybe it could be automated eventually," said Grant. "Perhaps little housekeeping robots can be sent in to clean up the mess. Or perhaps every human being in early manhood can be injected with a permanent supply of such vessel-cleansers—my God, look at the length of it."

They were closer still to the arterial wall now, and the ride was growing rougher in the turbulence near it. Looking ahead, though, they could see the wall stretching ahead for what seemed unbroken miles before veering off.

Michaels said, "The circulatory system, counting all its vessels to the very smallest, is, as I told you earlier, a hundred thousand miles long, if it were strung out in one long line."

"Not bad," said Grant.

"A hundred thousand miles in the *un*miniaturized scale. On our present scale, it is," he paused to think, then said, "over three trillion miles long—half a light year. To travel through every one of Benes' blood vessels in our present state would be almost the equivalent of a trip to a star."

He looked about haggardly. Neither their safety thus far, nor the beauty of their surroundings, seemed to have consoled him much.

Grant strove to be cheerful. "At least the Brownian motion isn't at all bad," he said.

"No," said Michaels. Then, "I didn't come off too well a while ago when we first discussed Brownian motion."

"Neither did Duval just now in the matter of samples. I don't think any of us are doing *really* well."

Michaels swallowed. "That was typically single-minded of Duval to want to stop for specimens."

He shook his head and turned to the charts on the curving desk against one wall. It, and the moving dot of light upon it, was a duplicate of the much larger version in the control tower, and of the smaller version in Owens' bubble. He said, "What's our speed, Owens?"

"Fifteen knots, our scale."

"Of course our scale," said Michaels, pettishly. He lifted his slide rule from its recess and made a rapid calculation. "We'll be at the branch in two minutes. Keep the wall at its present distance when you turn. That will bring you safely into the middle of the branch and you can then move smoothly into the capillary net without further branching. Is that clear?"

"All clear!"

Grant waited, watching always through the window. For a moment, he caught the shadow of Cora's profile and watched that, but the view from the window overpowered even his study of the curve of her chin.

Two minutes? How much would that be! Two minutes as his miniaturized time-sense would make it out to be? Or two minutes by their time-recorder? He twisted his head to look at it. It read 56 and, as he watched, it blanked out and then, very deliberately, 55 appeared dimly and darkened.

There was a sudden wrench and Grant was nearly thrown out of his seat.

"Owens!" he cried out. "What happened?"

Duval said, "Have we struck something?"

Grant struggled his way toward the ladder and managed to climb up. He said, "What's wrong?"

"I don't know." Owens' face was a contorted mass of effort. "The ship won't handle."

Michaels' voice came up tensely, "Captain Owens, correct your course. We're approaching the wall."

"I . . . know that," gasped Owens. "We're in some sort of current."

Grant said, "Keep trying. Do your best."

He swung down and, with his back against the ladder, trying to hold steady against the heaving of the ship, said, "Why should there be a cross-current here? Aren't we going along with the arterial flow?

"Yes," said Michaels, emphatically, his face waxen in its pallor, "there can't be anything to force us sideways like this." He pointed outward at the arterial wall, much closer now and still approaching. "There must be something wrong with the controls. If we strike the wall and damage it, a clot may form about us and fix us there, or the white cells may respond."

Duval said, "But this is impossible in a closed system. The laws of hydrodynamics . . ."

"A closed system?" Michaels' eyebrows shot upward. With an effort, he staggered his way to his charts, then moaned, "It's no use, I need more magnification and I can't get it here. For God's sake, Owens, keep away from the wall."

"Damn it, man," Owens shouted back, "I'm trying. I tell you there's a current that I can't fight."

"Don't try to fight it directly, then," cried Grant. "Give the ship its head and confine yourself to trying to keep its course parallel to the wall."

They were close enough now to see every detail of the wall. The strands of connective tissue that served as its chief support were like trusses, almost like Gothic arches, yellowish in color and glimmering with a thin layer of what seemed a fatty substance.

The connective strands stretched and bowed apart as though the whole structure were expanding, hovered a moment, then moved together again, the surface between the trusses crinkling as they closed in. Grant did not need to ask to realize he was watching the arterial wall pulse in time to the beat of the heart.

The buffeting of the ship was growing worse. The wall was closer still and beginning to look ragged. The connective strands had worked loose in spots, as though they themselves had been withstanding a raging torrent for much longer than even the *Proteus* had, and were beginning to buckle under the strain. They swayed like cables of a gigantic bridge, coming up to the window and sliding past wetly, giving off their sparkling yellow color in the jumping beam of the ship's headlights.

The approach of the next one made Cora scream in shrill terror.

Michaels shouted, "Watch *out*, Owens."

Duval muttered, "The artery is damaged."

But the current swept around the living buttress and carried the ship with it, throwing it into a sickening lurch that piled everyone helplessly against the left wall.

Grant, his left arm having withstood a painful slam, caught at Cora with his other and managed to keep her upright. Staring straight ahead, he was trying to make sense out of the sparkling light.

He shouted, "Whirlpool! Get into your seats, all of you. Strap yourselves in."

The formed particles, from red corpuscles down, were virtually motionless outside the window for the moment as all were caught in the same whirling current, while the wall blurred into yellow featurelessness.

Duval and Michaels struggled to their seats and wrenched at their harnesses.

Owens shouted, "Some sort of opening dead ahead."

Grant said urgently to Cora, "Come *on*. Pull yourself into your seat."

"I'm *trying*," she gasped.

Desperately, all but unable to keep his footing against the sharp swaying of the ship, Grant pushed her down and then reached for her harness.

It was quite too late. The *Proteus* was caught up in the whirlpool now and was lifted upward and round with the force of a carnival whip.

Grant managed to seize a stanchion by a reflex grab and reached out for Cora. She had been hurled to the floor. Her fingers curled over the arm of her chair, and strained uselessly.

They were not going to hold, Grant knew, and he reached for her desperately, but he was a good foot short. His own arm was slipping from the stanchion as he reached for her.

Duval was struggling uselessly in his own seat, but centrifugal pressure had him pinned. "Hold on, Miss Peterson. I will try to help."

With an effort he had reached his harness, while Michaels watched, eyes turning toward them in frozen helplessness, and Owens, pinned in his bubble, remained completely out of the picture.

Cora's legs lifted from the ground in response to the centrifugal effect. "I can't . . ."

Grant, out of sheer lack of alternatives, released his own hold. He slithered across the floor, hooked a leg around the base of a chair with a blow that numbed it, managed to transfer his left arm there, too, and with his right caught Cora about the waist as her own grip gave way.

The *Proteus* was turning faster, now, and seemed to be angling downward. Grant could stand the strained position of his body no longer and his leg flipped away from the chair leg. His arm, already bruised and painful by earlier contact with the wall, took the additional strain with an ache that made it feel as though it were breaking. Cora clutched at his shoulder and seized the material of his uniform with viselike desperation.

Grant managed to grunt out, "Has anyone . . . figured out what's happening?"

Duval, still struggling futilely with his harness, said, "It's a fistula—an arterio-venous fistula."

With an effort, Grant raised his head and looked out the window once more. The damaged arterial wall came to an end dead ahead. The yellow sparking ceased and a blackened ragged gap was visible. It reached as high and as low as his restricted vision could make out and red corpuscles, as well as other objects, were vanishing into it. Even the occasional, terrifying blobs of white cells were sucked rapidly through the hole.

"Just a few seconds," gasped Grant. "Just a few . . . Cora." He was telling it to himself, to his own aching, bruised arm.

With a final vibration that nearly stunned Grant with the agony he had to endure, they were through, and slowing, slowing, into sudden calm.

Grant released his hold and lay there, panting heavily. Slowly, Cora managed to get her legs under her and stand up.

Duval was free now. "Mr. Grant, how are you?" He knelt down at Grant's side.

Cora knelt down, too, touching Grant's arm gently, venturing to try to knead it. Grant grimaced in pain. "Don't touch it!"

"Is it broken?" asked Duval.

"I can't tell." Gingerly and slowly, he tried to bend it; then caught his left biceps in his right palm, and held it tightly.

"Maybe not. But even if it isn't, it will be weeks before I can do that again."

Michaels had also risen. His face was twisted almost unrecognizably by relief. "We made it. We made it. We're in one piece. How is it, Owens?"

"In good order, I think," said Owens. "Not a red light on the panel. The *Proteus* took more than it was designed to take and it held." His voice reflected a fierce pride in himself and his ship.

Cora was still brooding helplessly over Grant. She said, in shock, "You're bleeding!"

"I am? Where?"

"Your side. The uniform is showing blood."

"Oh, that. I had a little trouble on the Other Side. It's just a matter of replacing a band-aid. Honestly, it's nothing. Just blood."

Cora looked anxious, then unzipped his uniform. "Sit up," she said. "Please try to sit up." She slipped an arm under his shoulders and struggled him upright, then pulled the uniform down over his shoulders with practiced gentleness.

"I'll take care of it for you," she said, ". . . and thank you. It seems foolishly inadequate, but thank you."

Grant said, "Well, do the same for me some time, all right? Help me into my chair, will you?"

He struggled to his feet now, Cora helping him on one side, Michaels on the other. Duval, after one glance at them, had limped to the window.

Grant said, "Now what happened?"

Michaels said, "An arterio-ven . . . . well, put it this way. An abnormal connection existed between an artery and a small vein. It happens sometimes, usually as the result of physical trauma. It happened to Benes at the time he was hurt in the car, I suppose. It represents an imperfection, a kind of inefficiency, but in this case not a serious one. It's microscopic; a tiny eddy."

"A tiny eddy. This!"

"On our miniaturized scale, of course, it's a gigantic whirlpool."

"Didn't it show up on your charts of the circulatory system, Michaels?" asked Grant.

"It must have. I could probably find it here on the ship's chart, if I could magnify it sufficiently. The trouble is my initial analysis had to be made in three hours and I missed it. I have no excuse."

Grant said, "All right, it just means some lost time. Plot out an alternate route and get Owens started. What's the time, Owens?" He looked at the time-recorder automatically as he asked. He read: 52, and Owens said, "Fifty-two."

"Plenty of time," said Grant.

Michaels was staring at Grant with raised eyebrows. He said, "There's no time, Grant. You haven't grasped what's happened. We're finished. We've failed. We can't get to the clot any more, don't you understand? We must ask to be removed from the body."

Cora said in horror, "But it will be days before the ship can be miniaturized again. Benes will die."

"There's nothing to be done. We're heading into the jugular vein now. We can't go back through the fistula for we couldn't buck that current, even when the heart is in the diastolic stage, between beats. The only other route, the one in which we follow the venous current, leads through the heart, which is clear suicide."

Grant said, numbly, "Are you sure?"

Owens said, in a cracked, dull voice, "He's right, Grant. The mission has failed."

CHAPTER 10 HEART

A MODIFIED HELL had broken loose in the control tower. The blip indicating the ship had scarcely changed position on the overall screen but the coordinate pattern had been critically altered.

Carter and Reid turned at the sound of a monitor signal.

"Sir," the face on the screen was agitated. "*Proteus* off course. They've picked up a blip in Quadrant 23, Level B."

Reid rushed to the window overlooking the mapping room. There was nothing to see at that distance, of course, except heads bent over the charts in quite obviously electric concentration.

Carter reddened. "Damn it, don't give me that quadrant crap. Where are they?"

"In the jugular vein, sir, heading for the superior vena cava."

"In a *vein!*" For a moment, Carter's own veins were in alarming evidence. "What the thundering hell are they doing in a vein? *Reid!*" he thundered.

Reid hurried to him. "Yes, I heard."

"How did they get into a vein?"

"I've ordered the men at the chart to try to locate an arterio-venous fistula. They're rare and not easy to find."

"And what . . ."

"Direct connection between a small artery and a small vein. The blood seeps over from the artery to the vein and . . ."

"Didn't they know it was there?"

"Obviously not. And, Carter . . ."

"What?"

"It may have been a pretty violent affair on their scale. They may not have survived."

Carter turned to the bank of television screens. He punched the appropriate button. "Any new messages from the *Proteus*?"

"No, sir," came the quick answer.

"Well, get in touch with them, man! Get something out of them! And put it through to me directly."

There was an agonizing wait while Carter held his chest motionless for the space of three or four ordinary breaths. The word came through. "*Proteus* reporting, sir."

"Thank God for so much," muttered Carter. "State the message."

"They've passed through an arterio-venous fistula, sir. They cannot return and they cannot go ahead. They ask leave to be brought out, sir."

Carter brought both fists down upon the desk. "No! By thunder, no!"

Reid said, "But General, they're right."

Carter looked up at the time-recorder. It stood at 51. He said, through trembling lips, "They have fifty-one minutes and they'll stay there fifty-one minutes. When that thing there reads zero, we take them out. Not a minute before, unless the mission is accomplished."

"But it's hopeless, damn it. God knows how weakened their ship is. We'll be killing five men."

"Maybe. That's the chance they take and that's the chance e take. But it will be firmly recorded that we never gave up s long as the smallest mathematical chance of success re- nained."

Reid's eyes were cold and his very mustache bristled. "General, you're thinking of *your* record. If they die, sir, I'll testify that you kept them in past reasonable hope."

"I'll take that chance, too," said Carter. "Now you tell me — you're in charge of the medical division — why can't they move?"

"They can't go back through the fistula against the current. That's physically impossible no matter how many orders you give. The gradation of blood pressure is not under Army control."

"Why can't they find another route?"

"All routes from their present position to the clot lead through the heart. The turbulence of the heart passage would smash them to kindling in an instant and we can't take that chance."

"We . . ."

"We *can't,* Carter. Not because of the lives of the men, though that's reason enough. If the ship is smashed, we'll never get all of it out and eventually its fragments will deminiaturize and kill Benes. If we get the men out now we can try operating on Benes from outside."

"That's hopeless."

"Not as hopeless as our present situation."

For a moment, Carter considered. He said, quietly, "Colonel Reid, tell me. Without killing Benes, how long can we stop his heart?"

Reid stared. "Not for long."

"I know that. I'm asking you for a specific figure."

"Well, in his comatose state, and under hypothermic chilling, but allowing for the shaky condition of his brain, I would say no more than sixty seconds. On the outside."

Carter said, "The *Proteus* can plow through the heart in less than sixty seconds, can't it?"

"I don't know."

"They'll have to try, then. When we've eliminated the impossible, whatever remains, however risky, however slim a hope, is what we're going to try. What are the problems involved in stopping the heart?"

"None. It can be done with a bare bodkin, to quote Hamlet. The trick will be to start it again."

"That, my dear Colonel, is going to be your problem and your responsibility." He looked at the time-recorder, which read 50. "We're wasting time. Let's get on with it. Get your heart men into action and I'll have the men on the *Proteus* instructed."

*

The lights were on within the *Proteus*. Michaels, Duval, and Cora, looking disheveled, clustered about Grant.

Grant said, "And that's it. They're stopping Benes' heart by electric shock at the moment of our approach and they'll start it again when we emerge."

"Start it again!" exploded Michaels. "Are they mad? Benes can't take that in his condition."

"I suspect," said Grant, "they consider it the only chance the mission has of succeeding."

"If that's the only chance, then we've failed."

Duval said, "I've had experience with open-heart surgery, Michaels. It may be possible. The heart is tougher than we think. Owens, how long will it take us to pass through the heart?"

Owens looked down from the bubble. "I've been figuring out just that, Duval. If we have no delays, we can do it in from fifty-five to fifty-seven seconds."

Duval shrugged. "We'd have three seconds to spare."

Grant said, "Then we'd better get on with it."

Owens said, "We're drifting with the current toward the heart right now. I'll shift the engines into high. I need to test them, anyway. They took a bad beating."

A muted throb rose somewhat in pitch and the sensation of forward motion overlay the dull, erratic trembling of Brownian motion.

"Lights out," said Owens, "and we'd better relax while I baby this thing along."

And with lights out, all drifted to the window again, even Michaels.

The appearance of the world about them had changed completely. It was still blood. It still contained all the bits and pieces, all the fragments and molecular aggregates, the platelets and red blood corpuscles, but the difference . . . the difference . . .

This was the superior vena cava now, the chief vein coming from the head and neck, its oxygen supply consumed and gone. The red blood corpuscles were drained of oxygen and now contained hemoglobin itself, not oxyhemoglobin, that bright red combination of hemoglobin and oxygen. Hemoglobin itself was a bluish-purple, and in the erratic reflection of the miniaturized light waves from the ship, each corpuscle glittered in flashes of blue and green with a frequently interspersed purple. All else took on the tinge of these unoxygenated corpuscles.

The platelets slid by in shadow and twice the ship passed, at a most grateful distance, the ponderous heavings of a white blood cell, colored now in greenish-tinged cream.

Grant looked at Cora's profile once more, lifted, as it was, with almost worshipful reverence, and itself looking infinitely mysterious in shadowy blue. She was the ice-queen of some polar region lit by a blue-green aurora, Grant thought quixotically, and suddenly found himself empty and yearning.

Duval murmured, "Glorious!" But it was not at Cora that he was looking.

Michaels said, "Are you ready, Owens? I'm going to guide you through the heart."

He moved to his charts and put on a small, overhead light that instantly dimmed the murky blue that had just filled the *Proteus* with mystery.

"Owens," he called. "Heart chart A-2. Approach, right atrium. You have it?"

"Yes, I have."

Grant said, "Are we at the heart already?"

"Listen for yourself," said Michaels, testily. "Don't look. Listen!"

An unbreathing silence fell upon those within the *Proteus*. They could hear it, like the distant boom of artillery. It was only a rhythmic vibration of the floor of the ship, slow and measured, but growing louder. A dull thud, followed by a duller; a pause, then a repetition, louder, always louder.

"The heart!" said Cora. "It is."

"That's right," said Michaels, "slowed a great deal."

"And we don't hear it accurately," said Duval, with dissatisfaction. "The sound waves are too immense in themselves to affect our ear. They set up secondary vibrations in the ship but that's not the same thing. In a proper exploration of the body . . ."

"At some future time, Doctor," said Michaels.

"It sounds like cannon," said Grant.

"Yes, but it lays down quite a barrage; two billion heartbeats in three score years and ten," said Michaels. "More."

"And every beat," added Duval, "is the thin barrier separating us from Eternity, each giving us time to make our peace with . . ."

"These particular beats," said Michaels, "will send us straight to Eternity and give us no time at all. Shut up, all of you. Are you ready, Owens?"

"I am. At least I'm at the controls and I've got the chart before me. But how do I find my way through this?"

"We can't get lost, even if we try. We're in the superior vena cava now, at the point of junction with the inferior. Got it?"

"Yes."

"All right. In seconds, we'll be entering the right atrium, the first chamber of the heart — and they had better stop the heart, too. Grant, radio our position."

Grant was momentarily lost to all else in his fascination with the view ahead. The vena cava was the largest vein in the body, receiving in the final stretch of its tube all the blood from all the body but the lungs. And as it gave way to the atrium, it became a vast resounding chamber, the walls of which were lost to sight, so that the *Proteus* seemed to be within a dark, measureless ocean. The heartbeat was a slow, terrifying pound now, and at each steady thud the ship seemed to lift and tremble.

At Michaels' second call, Grant snapped back to life and turned to his radio transmitter.

Owens called out, "Tricuspid valve ahead."

The others looked ahead. At the end of a long, long corridor, they could see it in the far distance. Three sparkling red sheets, separating and billowing open as they moved away from the ship. An aperture yawned and grew larger while the cusps of the valve fluttered each to its respective side. There beyond it was the right ventricle, one of the two main chambers.

The blood stream moved into the cavity as though being pulled by a powerful suction. The *Proteus* moved with it so that the aperture approached and enlarged at a tremendous rate. The current was smooth, however, and the ship rode it with scarcely a tremor.

Then came the sound of the thunderous boom of the ventricles, the main, muscular chambers of the heart, as they contracted in systole. The leaves of the tricuspid valve ballooned back toward the ship, moving slowly shut, with a wet, smacking contact, that closed the wall ahead into a long vertical furrow that parted into two above.

It was the right ventricle that lay on the other side of the now closed valve. As that ventricle contracted, the blood could not regurgitate through the atrium and was forced instead into and through the pulmonary artery.

Grant called out above the reverberating boom, "One more heartbeat and that will be the last, they say."

Michaels said, "It had better be, or it's our last heartbeat, too. Shove on through, full speed, Owens, the instant the valve opens again."

There was firm determination in his face now, Grant noted absently — no fear at all.

*

The radioactive sensors that had hovered about Benes' head and neck were now clustered over his chest, over a region from which the thermal blanket had been folded back. The charts of the circulating system on the wall had expanded now in the region of the heart and showed only part of the heart, the right atrium. The blip that marked the position of the *Proteus* had moved smoothly down the vena cava into the lightly muscled atrium which had expanded as they entered, then contracted.

The ship had, in one bound, been pushed nearly the length of the atrium toward the tricuspid valve, which closed just as they were at its brink. On an oscilloscopic scanner, each heartbeat was being translated into a wavering electronic beam and it was watched narrowly.

The electro-shock apparatus was in position; and the electrodes hovered over Benes' breast.

The final heartbeat began. The electron beam on the oscilloscope began moving upward. The left ventricle was relaxing for another intake of blood and as it relaxed the tricuspid valve would open.

"Now," cried the technician at the heart indicator.

The two electrodes came down upon the chest, a needle on one of the dials of the heart console swung instantly into the red and a buzzer sounded urgently. It was flipped into silence. The oscilloscope record flattened out.

The message went up to the control tower in all its final simplicity, "Heartbeat stopped."

Carter grimly clicked the stop watch in his hands and the seconds began ticking off with unbearable speed.

*

Five pairs of eyes looked forward at the tricuspid valve. Owens' hand was set for acceleration. The ventricle was relaxing and the semilunar valve at the end of the pulmonary artery somewhere in there, must be creaking shut. No blood could return to the ventricle from the artery; the valve made sure of that. The sound of its closing filled the air with an unbearable vibration.

And as the ventricle continued to relax, blood had to enter from another direction, from the right atrium. The tricuspid valve, facing in the other direction, began to flutter open.

The mighty, puckered crack ahead began to broaden, to make a corridor, a larger corridor, a vast opening.

"Now," shouted Michaels. "Now! Now!"

His words were lost in the heartbeat and in the rise of the engines. The *Proteus* shot forward, through the opening and into the ventricle. In a few seconds that ventricle would contract and in the furious turbulence that would follow the ship would be crushed like a match box and they would all be dead — and three-quarters of an hour later Benes would be dead.

Grant held his breath. The diastolic beat rumbled into silence and now — nothing!

A deadly silence had fallen.

Duval cried, "Let me see!"

He was up the ladder and his head emerged into the bubble, the one spot within the ship from which a clear, unobstructed view to the rear was possible.

"The heart has stopped," he cried. "Come and see."

Cora took his place, and then Grant.

The tricuspid valve hung half-open and limp. On its inner surface were the tremendous connective fibers that bound it to the inner surface of the ventricle, fibers that pulled the valve-leaves back when the ventricle relaxed and that held them firmly in position when the contraction of the ventricle forced them together, preventing those leaves from pushing through altogether and making a reversed opening.

"The architecture is marvelous," said Duval. "It would be magnificent to see that valve close from this angle."

"If you were to see that sight now, Doctor, it would be your last," said Michaels. "Top speed, Owens, and bear to the left, for the semilunar valve. We have thirty seconds to get out of this deathtrap."

If it were a deathtrap, and undoubtedly it was, it was a somberly beautiful one. The walls were strutted with mighty fibers, dividing into roots that were firmly fixed to the distant walls. It was as though they saw in the distance a gigantic forest of gnarled, leafless trees writhing and riven into a complex design that strengthened and held firm the most vital muscle of the human body.

That muscle, the heart, was a double pump that had to beat from well before birth to the final moment before death and did so with unbroken rhythm, unwearying strength, under all conditions. It was the greatest heart in the animal kingdom. The heart of no other mammal beat more than a billion times or so before even the most delayed approach of death, but after a billion heartbeats the human being was merely in early middle age, in the prime of his strength and power. Men and women had lived long enough to experience well over three billion heartbeats.

Owens' voice broke in. "Only nineteen seconds to go, Dr. Michaels. I see no sign of the valve yet."

"Keep on, damn it. You're headed there. And it had better be open."

Grant said tensely, "There it is. Isn't that it? That opening?"

Michaels looked up from his chart to cast the most cursory glance. "Yes, it is. And it's partly open, too, enough for us. The systolic heartbeat was at the point of starting when the heart was shut down. Now, everyone, strap yourselves in tightly. We're slamming through that opening, but the heartbeat will be right behind us and when it comes . . ."

"If it comes," said Owens softly.

"When it comes," repeated Michaels, "there'll be a terrific surge of blood. We'll have to stay as far ahead of it as possible."

With determined desperation, Owens flashed the ship ahead for the tiny opening in the center of the crescent crack ("semilunar" for that reason) that marked the closed valve.

*

The operating room labored under a tense silence. The surgical team, hovering over Benes, was as motionless as he. Benes' cold body and stopped heart brought the aura of death close to everyone in that room. Only the restlessly quivering sensors remained as signs of life.

In the control room, Reid said, "They're obviously safe so far. They're through the tricuspid and are following a curved path aiming at the semilunar valve. That's deliberate, powered motion."

"Yes," said Carter, watching his stop watch in tense agony. "Twenty-four seconds left."

"They're almost there now."

"Fifteen seconds left," said Carter, inexorably.

The heart technicians at the electro-shock apparatus moved stealthily into position.

"Aiming straight into the semilunar valve."

"Six seconds left. Five. Four . . ."

"They're going through." And as he spoke, a warning buzzer, ominous as death, sounded.

"Revive heartbeat," came the word over one of the speakers, and a red button was pressed. A pacemaker went into action, and a rhythmic surge of potential made its appearance on an appropriate screen in the form of a pulsing swing of light.

The oscilloscope registering heartbeat remained dead. The pacemaker pulse was increased, while eyes watched tensely.

"It's *got* to start," said Carter, whose whole body tensed and pushed forward in muscular sympathy.

•

The *Proteus* entered the aperture, which looked like a pair of barely open lips curved in a gigantically pendulous smile. It scraped against the tough membrane above and below, hung back a moment as the engine roar raised its pitch in a temporarily vain attempt to free the ship of the sticky embrace — then lunged through.

"We're out of the ventricle," said Michaels, rubbing his forehead and then looking at his hand, which had come away wet, "and into the pulmonary artery. Continue at full speed, Owens. The heartbeat should start in three seconds."

Owens looked back. He alone could do so, the others being strapped helplessly in their seats, with forward vision only.

The semilunar valve was receding, still closed, with its fibers straining their points of attachments into suckers of tense tissue. With distance, the valve grew smaller, and was still closed.

Owens said, "The heartbeat isn't coming. It isn't . . . wait, wait. There it is." The two leaves of the valve were relaxing; the fibrous supports were falling back and their tense roots puckered and became flabby.

The aperture was gaping, the rush of blood was coming, and overtaking them was the gigantic "bar-room-m-m" of the systole.

The tidal wave of blood caught up with the *Proteus,* hurtling it forward at breakneck velocity.

CHAPTER 11 CAPILLARY

THE FIRST HEARTBEAT broke the spell in the control tower. Carter raised both hands in the air and shook them in mute invocation of the gods. "Made it, by thunder. Brought them through!"

Reid nodded. "You won that time, General. I wouldn't have had the nerve to order them through the heart."

The whites of Carter's eyes were bloodshot. "I didn't have the nerve *not* to order it. Now if they can hold up against the arterial flow . . ." His voice rang out into the transmitter. "Get into touch with the *Proteus* the moment their speed diminishes."

Reid said, "They're back in the arterial system, but they're not heading for the brain, you know. The original injection was into the systemic circulation, into one of the main arteries leading from the left ventricle to the brain. The pulmonary artery leads from the right ventricle — to the lungs."

"It means delay. I know that," said Carter. "But we still have time." He indicated the time-recorder, which read 48.

"All right, but we'd better switch the point of maximum concentration to the respiration center."

He made the appropriate change and the interior of the respiration post was visible on the monitor screen.

Reid said, "What's the respiration rate?"

"Back to six per minute, Colonel. I didn't think we were going to make it there for a second."

"Neither did we. Hold it steady. You're going to have to worry about the ship. It will be in your sector in no time."

"Message from the *Proteus*," came another voice. "ALL WELL — uh, sir? There's more, do you want it read?"

Carter scowled. "Of course, I want it read."

"Yes, sir. It says: WISH YOU WERE HERE AND I WERE THERE."

Carter said, "Well, you tell Grant that I would rather a hundred times he . . . no, don't tell him anything. Forget it."

*

The end of the heartbeat had brought the surge forward to a manageable velocity, and the *Proteus* was moving along smoothly again, smoothly enough to make it possible to feel the soft, erratic Brownian motion.

Grant welcomed that sensation, for it could be felt only in the quiet moments and it was those quiet moments that he craved.

They were all out of their harnesses again, and Grant, at the window, found the view essentially the same as in the jugular vein. The same blue-green-violet corpuscles dominated the scene. The distant walls were more corrugated, perhaps, with the lines lying in the direction of motion.

They passed an opening.

"Not that one," said Michaels at the console, where he labored painfully over his charts. "Can you follow my markings up there, Owens?"

"Yes, Doc."

"All right. Count the turnings as I mark them and then to the right here. Is that plain?"

Grant watched the subdivisions coming at briefer and briefer intervals, dividing off right and left, above and below, while the channel along which they cruised became narrower, the walls more plainly seen and closer at hand.

"I'd hate to get lost in this highway pattern," said Grant, thoughtfully.

"You can't get lost," said Duval. "All roads lead to the lungs in this part of the body."

Michaels' voice was growing monotonous. "Up and right now, Owens. Straight ahead and then, uh, fourth left."

Grant said, "No more arterio-venous fistulas, I hope, Michaels."

Michaels shrugged him off impatiently, too absorbed to say anything.

Duval said, "Not likely. To come across two by accident is asking too much of chance. Besides we're approaching the capillaries."

The velocity of the blood stream had fallen off tremendously and so had that of the *Proteus.*

Owens said, "The blood vessel is narrowing, Dr. Michaels."

"It's supposed to. The capillaries are the finest vessels of all; quite microscopic in size. Keep going, Owens."

In the light of the headbeam it could be seen that the walls, as they constricted inward, had lost their furrows and creases and were becoming smooth. Their yellowness faded into cream and then into colorlessness.

They were taking on an unmistakable mosaic pattern, broken into curving polygons, each with a slightly thickened area near the center.

Cora said, "How pretty. You can see the individual cells of the capillary wall. Look, Grant." Then, as though remembering, "How's your side?"

"It's all right. Fine, in fact. You put on a very efficient band-aid, Cora. We're still friendly enough for the use of Cora as your name, I hope?"

"I suppose it would be rather ungrateful of me to object to that."

"And useless, too."

"How's your arm?"

Grant touched it gingerly, "Hurts like the devil."

"I'm sorry."

"Don't be sorry. Just — when the time comes — be very, very grateful."

Cora's lips tightened a bit and Grant added hurriedly, "Just my poor way of being light-hearted. How do *you* feel?"

"Quite myself. My side feels a little stiff, but not bad. And I'm not offended. But listen, Grant."

"When you talk, Cora, I listen."

"Band-aids aren't the latest medical advance, you know, and they're not the universal panacea. Have you done anything about warding off infection?"

"I put on some iodine."

"Well, will you see a doctor when we get out?"

"Duval?"

"You know what I mean."

Grant said, "All right. I will."

He turned back to the sight of the cell-mosaic. The *Proteus* was creeping now, inching through the capillary. In the light of its headbeams, dim shapes could be seen through the cells.

Grant said, "The wall seems to be translucent."

"Not surprising," said Duval. "Those walls are less than one ten-thousandth of an inch thick. They're quite porous, too. Life depends on material getting through those walls and through the equally thin walls that line the alveoli."

"The which?"

For a moment, he looked at Duval in vain. The surgeon

seemed more interested in what he was looking at than in Grant's question. Cora hastened to fill the gap.

She said, "Air enters the lungs through the trachea; you know — the windpipe. That divides, just as the blood vessels do, into smaller and smaller tubes until they finally reach the microscopic little chambers deep in the lung, where the air that enters finds itself separated from the interior of the body only by a narrow membrane, a membrane as narrow as that of the capillaries. Those chambers are the alveoli. There are about six hundred million of them in the lungs."

"Complicated mechanism."

"A magnificent one. Oxygen leaks across the alveolar membrane and across the capillary membrane, too. It finds itself in the blood stream and before it can leak back, the red blood corpuscles have picked it up. Meanwhile carbon dioxide wastes leak out in the other direction from blood to lungs. Dr. Duval is waiting to watch that happen. That's why he didn't answer."

"No excuses are necessary. I know what it is to be absorbed in one thing to the exclusion of another." He grinned broadly. "I'm afraid, though, that Dr. Duval's absorptions are not mine."

Cora looked uncomfortable, but a cry from Owens blocked off her answer.

"Straight ahead!" he called. "Watch what's coming."

All eyes turned ahead. A blue-green corpuscle was bumping along ahead of them, scraping its edges slowly against the walls of the capillary on either side. A wave of faint straw made its appearance at the edges and then swept inward, until all the darker color was gone.

Other blue-green corpuscles making their way past them turned color likewise. The headlights were picking up only straw color ahead and the color deepened into orange-red in the distance.

"You see," said Cora, excitedly, "as they pick up the oxygen, the hemoglobin turns into oxyhemoglobin and the blood brightens to red. That will be taken back to the left ventricle of the heart now and the rich, oxygenated blood will be pumped all over the body."

"You mean we have to go back through the heart again," said Grant, in instant concern.

"Oh, no," said Cora. "Now that we're in the capillary system, we'll be able to cut across." She didn't sound very certain of it, however.

Duval said, "Look at the wonder of it. Look at the God-given wonder of it."

Michaels said stiffly, "It's just a gas exchange. A mechanical process worked out by the random forces of evolution over a period of three billion years."

Duval turned fiercely. "Are you maintaining that this is accidental; that this marvelous mechanism, geared to perfection at a thousand points and all interlocking with clever certainty, is produced by nothing more than just the here-and-there collision of atoms?"

"That's exactly what I want to tell you. Yes," said Michaels.

At which point both, facing each other in belligerent exasperation, looked up with a snap at the sudden, raucous sound of a buzzer.

Owens said, "What the devil . . ."

He flicked at a switch desperately but a needle on one of his gauges was dropping rapidly toward a red horizontal line. He shut off the buzzer and called out, "Grant!"

"What is it?"

"Something's wrong. Check the Manual right over there."

Grant followed the pointing finger, moving quickly, while Cora crowded behind.

Grant said, "There's a needle in the red danger zone under something marked TANK LEFT. Obviously, the left tank's losing pressure."

Owens groaned and looked behind. "And how. We're bubbling air into the blood stream. Grant, get up here quickly." He was shucking his harness.

Grant scrambled toward the ladder, making room as best he might for Owens to squeeze past on the way down.

Cora managed to make out the bubbles through the small rear window. She said, "Air bubbles in the blood stream can be fatal . . ."

"Not this kind," said Duval hastily. "On our miniaturized scale we produce bubbles that are too tiny to do harm."

"Never mind the danger to Benes," said Michaels grimly. "*We* need the air."

Owens called back to Grant, who was seating himself at the controls. "Just leave everything as it is for now, but watch for any red signal flashes anywhere on the board."

He said to Michaels as he passed him, "There must be a frozen valve. I can't think of anything else."

He moved back and opened a panel with a quick wrench at one end, using a small tool he had removed from the pocket of his uniform. The maze of wires and circuit breakers was revealed in frightening complexity.

Owens' skilled fingers probed through them quickly, testing and eliminating with an ease and celerity that could only have marked the ship's designer. He tripped a switch, opened it quickly and let it snap shut, then moved forward to look over the auxiliary controls underneath the windows at the bow of the ship.

"There must have been some damage outside when we scraped into the pulmonary artery, or when the arterial blood surge hit us."

"Is the valve usable?" asked Michaels.

"Yes. It was jarred a little out of alignment, I think, and when something forced it open just now, maybe just one of the pushes of Brownian movement, it stayed that way. I've realigned it now and it will give no further trouble, only . . ."

"Only what?" said Grant.

"I'm afraid this has torn it. We don't have enough air to complete the journey. If this were an orthodox submarine, I'd say we would have to surface to renew the air supply."

"But then what do we do now?" asked Cora.

"Surface. It's all we can do. We've got to ask to be taken out right now or the ship becomes unmaneuverable in ten minutes and we strangle in five more."

He moved to the ladder. "I'll take over, Grant. You get to the transmitter and give them the news."

Grant said, "Wait. Do we have any reserve air?"

"That was it. All of it. All gone. In fact, when that air deminiaturizes, it will be much larger in volume than Benes. It will kill him."

"No, it won't," said Michaels. "The miniaturized molecules of the air we've lost will pass right through the tissues and out into the open. Very little will be left in the body by deminiaturization time. Still, I'm afraid Owens is right. We can't go on."

"But *wait*," said Grant. "Why can't we surface?"

"I've just said . . ." began Owens, impatiently.

"I don't mean, be taken out of here. I mean, *really* surface. There. Right there. We have blood corpuscles picking up oxygen in front of our eyes. Can't we do the same? There are only two thin membranes between ourselves and an ocean of air. Let's get it."

Cora said, "Grant's right."

"No, he isn't," said Owens. "What do you think we are? We're miniaturized with lungs the size of a bacterial fragment. The air on the other side of those membranes is unminiaturized. Each oxygen molecule in that air is almost large enough to see, damn it. Do you think we can take them into our lungs?"

Grant looked nonplused. "But . . ."

"We can't wait, Grant. You'll have to get in touch with the control room."

Grant said, "Not yet. Didn't you say this ship was originally meant for deep-sea research? What was it supposed to do underwater?"

"We were hoping to miniaturize underwater specimens for carriage to the surface and investigation at leisure."

"Well, then, you must have miniaturization equipment on board. You didn't pull it out last night, did you?"

"Of course we have it. But only on a small scale."

"How large scale do we need it? If we lead air into the miniaturizer, we can reduce the size of the molecules and lead them into our air tanks."

"We don't have the time for that," put in Michaels.

"If time runs out, then we'll ask to be taken out. Until then, let's try. You've got a snorkel on board, I suppose, Owens?"

"Yes." Owens seemed completely confused at Grant's rapid and urgent sentences.

"And we can run such a snorkel through the capillary and lung walls without harming Benes, can't we?"

"At our size, I should certainly think so," said Duval.

"All right then, we run the snorkel from lung to ship's miniaturizer and lead a tube from miniaturizer to the air-reserve chamber. Can you improvise that?"

Owens considered for a moment, seemed to catch fire at the prospect and said, "Yes, I think so."

"When Benes inhales, there'll be pressure enough to fill our tanks for us. Remember that time distortion will make our few minutes' grace seem longer than it is on the unminiaturized scale. Anyway, we've got to try."

Duval said, "I agree. We must try. By all means. *Now!*"

Grant said, "Thanks for the support, Doctor."

Duval nodded, then said, "What's more, if we're going to try this, let's not try to make a one-man job out of it. Owens had better stay at the controls, but I will come out with Grant."

"Ah," said Michaels. "I was wondering what you were after. I see now. You want a chance at exploration in the open."

Duval flushed, but Grant broke in hastily, "Whatever the motive, the suggestion is good. In fact, we had better all come out. Except Owens, of course. The snorkel is aft, I suppose."

"In the supply and storage compartment," said Owens. He was back at the controls now, staring straight ahead. "If you've ever seen a snorkel, you won't mistake it."

Grant moved hastily into the compartment, saw the snorkel at once and reached for the packaged underwater gear.

Then he stopped in horror and shouted, "Cora!"

She was behind him in a moment. "What's the matter?"

Grant tried not to explode. It was the first time he looked at the girl without an appreciative inner comment on her beauty. For the moment, he was merely agonized. He pointed and said, "Look at that!"

She looked and turned a white face toward him. "I don't understand."

The laser over the working counter was swinging loose on one hook, its plastic cover off.

"Didn't you bother securing it?" demanded Grant.

Cora nodded wildly. "I did! I *did* secure it! I swear it. Heavens . . ."

"Then how could it . . ."

"I don't *know*. How can I answer that?"

Duval was behind her, his eyes narrowed and his face hard. He said, "What has happened to the laser, Miss Peterson?"

Cora turned to meet the new questioner. "I don't know. Why do you all turn on me? I'll test it right now. I'll check . . ."

"No!" roared Grant. "Just put it down and make sure it

won't knock around any further. We've got to get our oxygen before we do anything else."

He began handing out the suits.

Owens had come down from the bubble. He said, "The ship's controls are locked in place. We won't be going anywhere here in the capillary anyway . . . my God, the laser!"

"Don't you start," screamed Cora, eyes now swimming in tears.

Michaels said, clumsily, "Now, Cora, it won't help if you break down. Later, we'll consider this carefully. It must have been knocked loose in the whirlpool. Clearly an accident."

Grant said, "Captain Owens, connect this end of the snorkel to the miniaturizer. The rest of us will get into our suits and I hope someone shows me quickly how to get into mine. I've never tried this."

*

Reid said, "There's no mistake? They're not moving?"

"No, sir," came the technician's voice. "They're on the outer limits of the right lung and they're staying there."

Reid turned to Carter. "I can't explain it."

Carter stopped his angry pacing for a moment and jerked a thumb at the time-recorder, which was reading 42. "We've killed over a quarter of all the time available and we're farther from that damn clot than when we started. We should have been out by now."

"Apparently," said Reid, coldly, "we are laboring under a curse."

"And I don't feel whimsical about it, either, Colonel."

"Nor do I. But what am I supposed to feel in order to satisfy you?"

"At least, let's find out what's holding them up." He closed the appropriate circuit and said, "Contact the *Proteus*."

Reid said, "I suppose it's some sort of mechanical difficulty."

"You suppose!" said Carter, with urgent sarcasm. "I don't suppose they've just stopped for a quiet swim."

CHAPTER 12 LUNG

THE FOUR OF THEM, Michaels, Duval, Cora, and Grant, were in their swim suits now, form-fitting, comfortable, and in antiseptic white. Each had oxygen cylinders strapped to the back, a flashlight on the forehead, fins on the feet, and a radio transmitter and receiver at mouth and ear respectively.

"It's a form of skin-diving," said Michaels, adjusting the headgear, "and I've never gone skin-diving. To have the first try at it in someone's blood stream . . ."

The ship's wireless tapped urgently.

Michaels said, "Hadn't you better answer that?"

"And get into a conversation?" said Grant, impatiently. "There'll be time for talk when we're done. Here, help me."

Cora guided the plastic-shielded helmet over Grant's head and snapped it into place.

Grant's voice, transmuted at once into the faintly distorted version that comes over a small radio, sounded in her ear, "Thanks, Cora."

She nodded at him dolefully.

One by one they used the escape hatch. Precious air had to be consumed by forcing blood plasma out of the hatch each time.

Grant found himself paddling in a fluid that was not even as clear as the water one would find on the average polluted beach. It was full of floating debris, flecks, and bits of matter. The *Proteus* filled half the diameter of the capillary and past it red blood corpuscles nudged their way. Periodically, smaller platelets passed, with more room to spare.

Grant said uneasily, "If platelets break against the *Proteus,* we may form a clot."

"We may," said Duval, "but it won't be dangerous here; not in a capillary."

They could see Owens within the ship. He lifted his head and revealed an anxious face. He nodded and moved his hand without enthusiasm, trying to dodge and turn so as to be visible between and among the endlessly passing corpuscles. He put on the headgear of his own swimsuit and spoke into its transmitter.

He said, "I think I've got it arranged here. Anyway, I've done my best. Are you ready to have me release the snorkel?"

"Go ahead," said Grant.

It came out of the special release hatch like a cobra coming out of a fakir's basket at the sound of the pipes.

Grant seized it.

Michaels said, "Oh, hell," in a sort of whisper. Then, more loudly, and in a tone that seemed saturated with chagrin, he said, "Consider how narrow the bore of that snorkel is, all of you. It looks as big around as a man's arm, but how big is a man's arm on our scale?"

"What of it?" said Grant, shortly. He had a firm grip on the snorkel now and he put his back into moving with it toward the capillary wall, disregarding the soreness of his left biceps. "Grab hold, will you, and help pull."

Michaels said, "There's no point to it. Don't you understand? It should have occurred to me sooner, but the air won't go through that thing."

"What?"

"Not quickly enough. Unminiaturized air molecules are quite big compared to the opening in that snorkel. Do you expect air to leak through a tiny tube that you could barely see through a microscope?"

"The air will be under lung-pressure."

"So what? Ever hear of a slow leak in an automobile tire? The hole through which air leaks in such a tire is probably no smaller than that and is under considerably more pressure than the lung can generate, and it's a *slow* leak. Hell," and Michaels grimaced lugubriously. "I wish I had thought of this sooner."

Grant roared, "Owens!"

"I hear you. Don't crack every eardrum in existence."

"Never mind hearing me. Did you hear Michaels?"

"Yes, I did."

"Is he right? You're the nearest thing to a miniaturization expert we have. Is he right?"

"Well, yes and no," said Owens.

"And what the devil does that mean?"

"It means, yes, the air will go through the snorkel only very slowly unless it is miniaturized and, no, we need not worry if I can succeed in miniaturizing it. I can extend the field through the snorkel and miniaturize the air on the other side and suck that through by . . ."

"Won't such a field-extension affect us?" put in Michaels.

"No, I'll have it set for a fixed maximum of miniaturization and we're there already."

"How about the surrounding blood and lung tissue?" asked Duval.

"There's a limit to how sharply selective I can make the

field," admitted Owens. "This is only a small miniaturizer I have here, but I can confine it to gas, that is, to substances of low density. There's bound to be some damage however. I just hope it won't be too much."

"We'll have to chance it, that's all," said Grant. "Let's get on with it. We can't take forever."

With four pairs of arms encircling the snorkel and four pairs of legs pumping away, it reached the capillary wall.

For a moment, Grant hesitated. "We're going to have to cut through. Duval!"

Duval's lips curved in a small smile. "There's no need to call on the surgeon. At this microscopic level, you would do as well. There is no skill needed."

He drew a knife from a small scabbard at his waist, and looked at it. "It undoubtedly has miniaturized bacteria on it. Eventually, they will deminiaturize in the blood stream but the white cells will take care of them, then. Nothing pathogenic in any case, I hope."

"Please get on with it, Doctor," said Grant, urgently.

Duval slashed neatly with his knife between two of the cells that made up the capillary. A neat slit opened. The thickness of the wall might be a ten-thousandth of an inch in the world generally, but on their own miniaturized scale the thickness amounted to several yards. Duval stepped into the slit and forced his way through, breaking strands of intercellular cement and cutting farther. The wall was perforated at last and the cells drew apart, like the lips of a gaping wound.

Through the wound could be seen another set of cells, at which Duval slashed neatly and with precision.

He returned and said, "It's a microscopic opening. There'll be no loss of blood to speak of."

"No loss at all," said Michaels emphatically. "The leakage is the other way."

And, indeed, a bubble of air seemed to bulge inward at the opening. It bulged farther and then stopped.

Michaels put his hand to the bubble. A portion of its surface pushed inward, but the hand did not go through.

"Surface tension!" he said.

"What now?" demanded Grant.

"Surface tension, I tell you. At any liquid surface there is a kind of skin effect. To something as large as a human being, an unminiaturized human being, the effect is too small to be noticed, but insects can walk on water surfaces because of it. In our miniaturized state, the effect is even stronger. We may not be able to get beyond the barrier."

Michaels drew his knife and plunged it into the fluid-gas interface as, a moment before, Duval had operated on the cells. The knife forced the interface forward into a point, then broke through.

"It's like cutting thin rubber," said Michaels, panting a bit. He sliced downward, and an opening appeared briefly but closed almost at once, healing itself.

Grant tried the same thing, forcing his hand through the opening before it closed. He winced a bit as the water molecules closed in.

"It's got a grip on it, you know."

Duval said somberly, "If you calculated the size of those water molecules on our scale you'd be astonished. You could make them out with a hand lens. In fact . . ."

Michaels said, "In fact, you're sorry you didn't bring a hand lens. I've got news for you, Duval, you wouldn't see much. You would magnify the wave properties as well as the particle properties of atoms and subatomic particles. Anything you see, even by the reflection of miniaturized light, would be too hazy to do you much good."

Cora said, "Is that why nothing really looks sharp? I thought it was just because we were seeing things through blood plasma."

"The plasma is a factor, certainly. But in addition, the general graininess of the universe becomes much larger as we become much smaller. It's like looking really closely at an old-fashioned newspaper photograph. You see the dots more clearly and it becomes hazy."

Grant was paying little attention to the conversation. His arm was through the interface and with it he was tearing away to make room for his other arm and his head.

For a moment the fluid closed about his neck and he felt strangled.

"Hold my legs, will you?" he called.

Duval said, "I've got them."

Half his body was through now and he could look through the crevice Duval had made through the walls.

"All right. Pull me down again." He came down and the interface closed behind him with a popping sound.

He said, "Now let's see what we can do about the snorkel. Heave-ho."

It was quite useless. The blunt end of the snorkel made not a dent on the tightly knit skin of water molecules on the air bubble. Knives cut that skin to shreds so that parts of the snorkel got through but the instant the interface was left to itself, surface tension would take over and the snorkel would pop out.

Michaels was panting with effort. "I don't think we're going to make it."

"We've got to," said Grant. "Look, I'm getting in; all the way in. When you push the snorkel through, I'll grab whatever part makes it and pull. Between pushing and pulling . . ."

"You can't go in there, Grant," said Duval. "You'll be sucked in and lost."

Michaels said, "We can use a lifeline. Right here, Grant."

He indicated the neatly nested line at Grant's left hip. "Duval, take this back to the ship and attach it and we'll get Grant through."

Duval took the end handed him, rather uncertainly, and swam back toward the ship.

Cora said, "But how will you get back? Suppose you can't push through the surface tension again?"

"Sure, I will. Besides, don't confuse the situation by taking up problem number two while problem number one is still with us."

Owens, within the ship, watched tensely as Duval swam up. "Do you need another pair of hands out there?" he asked.

Duval said, "I don't think so. Besides, your pair is needed at the miniaturizer." He hitched the safety line to a small ring on the ship's metal skin and waved his arm. "O.K., Grant."

Grant waved back. His second penetration of the interface was more quickly done, for he had the knack now. First a slit, then one arm (ouch, the bruised bicep), then the other; then a strenuous push against the interface with his arms, and a kick with his finned legs and he popped out like a watermelon seed from between finger and thumb.

He found himself between the two sticky walls of the intercellular slit. He looked down at Michaels' face, clearly visible but somewhat distorted through the curve of the interface.

"Push it through, Michaels."

Through the interface, he could make out a thrashing of limbs, the swing of an arm holding a knife. And then the blunt metal end of the snorkel made a partial appearance. Grant knelt and seized it. Bracing his back against one side of the crevice and his feet against the other, he pulled. The interface rose with it, clinging to it all about. Grant worked his way upward ahead of it, gasping out, "Push! Push!"

It broke through, clear at last. Inside the tube of the snorkel was fluid, clinging motionlessly.

Grant said, "I'm going to get it up through now, into the alveolus."

Michaels said, "When you get to the alveolus, be careful. I don't know how you'll be affected by inhalation and exhalation but you're liable to find yourself in a hurricane."

Grant was moving upward, yanking at the snorkel as he found purchases for gripping fingers and kicking feet in the soft, yielding tissue.

His head rose beyond the alveolar wall and quite suddenly, he was in another world. The light from the *Proteus* penetrated through what seemed to him a vast thickness of tissue and in its muted intensity, the alveolus was a tremendous cavern, with walls that glinted moistly and distantly.

About him were crags and boulders of all sizes and colors, sparkling iridescently as the inefficient reflection of miniaturized light gave them all a spuriously beautiful luster. He could see now that the edges of the boulders remained hazy even without the presence of slowly swirling fluid to account for it.

Grant said, "This place is full of rocks."

"Dust and grit, I imagine," came Michaels' voice. "Dust and grit. The legacy of living in civilization, of breathing unfiltered air. The lungs are a one-way passage; we can take dust in but there's no way of pushing it out again."

Owens put in, "Do your best to hold the snorkel over your head, will you? I don't want any fluid plugging it — now!"

Grant heaved it high. "Let me know when you've had enough, Owens," he panted.

"I will."

"Is it working?"

"It sure is. I have the field adjusted strobophilically so that it acts in rapid spurts according to the . . . well, never mind. The point is the field is never on long enough to affect liquids or solids significantly but it is miniaturizing gases at a great rate. I've got the field extended far beyond Benes into the atmosphere of the operating room."

"Is that safe?" asked Grant.

"It's the only way we can get enough air. We have to have thousands of times as much air as all of Benes' lungs contain, and miniaturize it all. Is it safe? Good lord, man, I'm sucking it in right through Benes' tissues without even affecting his respiration. Oh, if I only had a larger snorkel." Owens sounded as gay and excited as a youngster on his first date.

Michaels' voice in Grant's ear said, "How are you being affected by Benes' breathing?"

Grant looked quickly at the alveolar membrane. It seemed stretched and taut under his foot, so he guessed he was witnessing the slow, slow end of an inhalation. (Slow in any case; slower because of the hypothermia; slower still because of the time-distortion induced by miniaturization.)

"It's all right," he said. "No effect at all."

But now a low rasp made itself felt in Grant's ear. It grew slowly louder and Grant realized an exhalation was beginning. He braced himself and held on to the snorkel.

Owens said jubilantly, "This is working beautifully. Nothing like this has ever been done before."

The motion of air was making itself felt about Grant, as the lungs continued their slow but accelerating collapse and the rasp of exhalation grew louder. Grant felt his legs lifting from the alveolar floor. On an ordinary scale, he knew, the air current in the alveolus was indetectably gentle, but on the miniaturized scale, it was gathering into a tornado.

Grant gripped the snorkel in desperation, flinging both arms about it and both legs. It strained upward and so did he. The very boulders — dust-boulders — came loose and rolled slightly.

The wind slowly died then as the exhalation came to its slow halt and Grant released the snorkel with relief.

He said, "How's it doing, Owens?"

"Almost done. Hang on for a few seconds, will you, Grant?"

"Okay."

He counted to himself: twenty . . . thirty . . . forty. The inhalation was starting and air molecules were impinging upon him. The alveolar wall was stretching again and he stumbled to his knees.

"Full!" cried Owens. "Get back in."

"Pull down on the snorkel," yelled Grant. "Quickly. Before another exhalation comes."

He pushed downward and they pulled. Difficulty arose only when the lip of the snorkel approached the interface. It held tight there for a moment as though in a vise, and then pulled through with a small thunderclap of joining surface film.

Grant had watched too long. With the snorkel safely in, he made a motion as though to plunge into the crevice and through the interface at its bottom, but the beginning of the exhalation surrounded him with wind and caused him to stumble. For a moment, he was wedged between two dust-boulders and he found that in wrenching free he had slightly barked one shin. (Hurting one's shin against a particle of dust was surely something to tell one's grandchildren.)

Where was he? He shook his lifeline, freeing it from some snag on one of the boulders, and pulled it taut. It would be easiest to follow it back to the crevice.

The lifeline snaked over the top of the boulder and Grant, bracing his feet against it, climbed rapidly upward. The strengthening exhalation helped him do so and there was scarcely any sensation of effort in the upward striving. Then still less. The crevice, he knew, was just the other side of the boulder and he might have gone about it but for the fact that the exhalation made the route over it the simpler and because (why not admit it?) it was more exciting this way.

The boulder rolled beneath his feet, at the peak of the exhalation wind, and Grant lifted free. For a moment he found himself high in the air, the crevice just beyond, exactly where he had expected it to be. It was only necessary to wait a second or two for exhalation to cease and he would lunge quickly for the crevice, the blood stream, and the ship.

And even as he thought so, he felt himself sucked wildly upward, the lifeline following and whipping entirely free of the crevice which, in half a moment, was lost to sight.

*

The snorkel had been pulled out of the alveolar crevice and Duval was getting it back to the ship.

Cora said anxiously, "Where's Grant?"

"He's up there," said Michaels, peering.

"Why doesn't he come down?"

"He will. He will. It takes some negotiating, I imagine." He peered upward again. "Benes is exhaling. Once that's done, he'll have no trouble."

"Shouldn't we grab hold of his lifeline and pull him in?"

Michaels threw out an arm and forestalled her. "If you do that and yank just as an inhalation starts, forcing him downward, you may hurt him. He'll tell us what to do if he needs help."

Restlessly, Cora watched and then broke away toward the lifeline. "Now," she said, "I want to . . ."

And at that moment the lifeline twitched and snaked upward, its end flashing past, and out through the opening.

Cora screamed, and kicked herself desperately toward the opening.

Michaels pursued. "You can't do anything," he panted. "Don't be foolish."

"But we can't leave him in there. What will happen to him?"

"We'll hear from him by his radio."

"It may be broken."

"Why should it be?"

Duval joined them. He said, chokingly, "It came loose as I watched. I couldn't believe it."

All three gazed upward helplessly.

Michaels called, tentatively, "Grant! Grant! Do you receive me?"

*

Grant went tumbling and twisting upward, the useless lifeline still attached to his belt and whipping behind him. His thoughts were as jumbled as his line of flight.

I won't get back, was the dominant thought. I won't get back. Even if I stay in radio contact, I can't come in on the beam.

Or could he?

"Michaels," he called. "Duval."

There was nothing at first, then a faint, crackling noise in his ears, and a distorted squawk that might have been "Grant!"

He tried again, "Michaels! Do you hear me? Do you hear me?"

Again the squawking. He could not make out anything.

Somewhere within a tense mind there came a calm thought, as though his intellect had found time to make a serene note. Although miniaturized light waves were more penetrating than the ordinary kind, miniaturized radio waves seemed less penetrating.

Very little was known about the miniaturized state, apparently. It was the misfortune of the *Proteus* and her crew to be pioneers into a realm that was literally unknown; surely a fantastic voyage if ever there was one.

And within that voyage, Grant was now on a fantastic subvoyage of his own, blown through what seemed miles of space within a microscopic air-chamber in the lung of a dying man.

His motion was slowing. He had reached the top of the

alveolus and had moved into the tubular stalk from which it was suspended. The far-off light of the *Proteus* was dim indeed.

Could he follow the light, then? Could he try to move in whatever direction it seemed stronger?

He touched the wall of the tubular stalk and stuck there, like a fly on flypaper. And with no more sense than the fly, at first, he wriggled.

Both legs and an arm were stuck to the wall in no time. He paused and forced himself to think. Exhalation was complete but inhalation would be beginning. The air current would be forcing him downward. Wait for it!

He felt the wind begin and heard the rushing noise. Slowly, he pulled his clinging arm loose and bent his body out into the wind. It pushed him downward and his legs came loose, too.

He was falling now, plunging downward from a height which, on his miniaturized scale, was mountainous. From the unminiaturized point of view, he knew he must be drifting downward in feathery fashion, but as it was, what he experienced was a plummet. It was a smooth drop, non-accelerated, for the large molecules of air (almost large enough to see, Michaels had said) had to be pushed to one side as he fell, and that took the energy that would otherwise have gone into acceleration.

A bacterium, no larger than he, could fall this distance safely, but he, the miniaturized human, was made up of fifty trillion miniaturized cells and that complexity made him fragile enough, perhaps, to smash apart into miniaturized dust.

Automatically, as he thought that, he threw up his hands in self-defense when the alveolar wall came whirling close. He felt the glancing contact; the wall gave soggily and he bounced off after clinging for a moment. His speed of fall had actually slowed.

Down again. Somewhere below, a speck of light, a bare pinpoint had winked on as he watched. He kept his eye fixed on that with a wild hope.

Still down. He kicked his feet wildly to avoid an outcropping of dust-boulders. He narrowly missed them and struck a spongy area again. Again falling. He thrashed wildly in an attempt to move toward the pinpoint of light as he fell and it seemed to him he may have succeeded somewhat. He wasn't sure.

He came rolling down the lower slope of the alveolar surface at length. He flung his lifeline around an outcropping and just barely held on.

The pinpoint of light had become a small glare, some fifty feet away, he judged. That *must* be the crevice, and close though it was, he couldn't possibly have found it without the guidance of the light.

He waited for the inhalation to cease. In the short interval of time before exhalation, he had to make it there.

Before inhalation had come to a complete halt, he was slipping and scrambling across the space between. The alveolar membrane stretched in the final moment of inhalation and then, hovering at that point for a couple of seconds, began to lose its tension as the first instants of gathering exhalation began.

Grant threw himself down the crevice, which was ablaze with light. He kicked at the interface, which rebounded in rubbery fashion. A knife slit through; a hand appeared and seized his ankle in firm grip. He felt the pull downward just as the upward draft was beginning to make itself felt about his ears.

Down he went, with other hands adding to the grip on his legs, and he was back in the capillary. Grant breathed in long, shuddering gasps. Finally, he said, "Thanks! I followed the light! Couldn't have made it otherwise."

Michaels said, "Couldn't reach you by radio."

Cora was smiling at him. "It was Dr. Duval's idea. He had the *Proteus* move up to the opening and shine its headlight directly into it. And he made the opening bigger, too."

Michaels said, "Let's get back in the ship. We've lost just about all the time we can afford to lose."

CHAPTER 13 PLEURA

REID CRIED OUT, "A message is coming through, Al."

"From the *Proteus?*" Carter ran to the window.

"Well, not from your wife."

Carter waved his hand impatiently. "Later. Later. Save all the jokes and we'll go over them one by one in a big heap. Okay?"

The word came through: "Sir, *Proteus* reports DANGEROUS AIR LOSS. REFUELING STOP CARRIED THROUGH SUCCESSFULLY."

"Refueling?" cried Carter.

Reid said, frowning, "I suppose they mean the lungs. They're at the lungs, after all, and that means cubic miles of air on their scale. But . . ."

"But what?"

"They can't use that air. It's unminiaturized."

Carter looked at the colonel in exasperation. He barked into the transmitter. "Repeat the last sentence of the message."

"REFUELING STOP CARRIED THROUGH SUCCESSFULLY."

"Is that last word 'successfully'?"

"Yes, sir."

"Get in touch with them and confirm."

He said to Reid, "If they say 'successfully,' I suppose they handled it."

"The *Proteus* has a miniaturizer on board."

"Then that's how they did it. We'll get an explanation afterward."

The voice came up from communications. "Message confirmed, sir."

"Are they moving?" asked Carter, making another connection.

A short pause and then, "Yes, sir. They're moving through the pleural lining."

Reid nodded his head. He looked up at the time-recorder, which read 37, and said, "The pleural lining is a double membrane surrounding the lungs. They must be moving in the space between; a clear road, an expressway really, right to the neck."

"And they'll be where they started half an hour ago," grated Carter. "Then what?"

"They can back into a capillary and find their way to the carotid artery again, which is time consuming; or they may bypass the arterial system by taking to the lymphatics, which involves other problems. Michaels is the pilot; I suppose he'll know what to do."

"Can you advise him? For God's sake, don't rest on protocol."

Reid shook his head. "I'm not sure which course is wisest, and he's on the scene. He'll be a better judge as to how well the ship can withstand another arterial battering. We've got to leave it to them, General."

"I wish I knew what to do," said Carter. "By the lord, I'd take the responsibility, if I knew enough to do so with a reasonable chance of success."

"But that's exactly how I feel," said Reid, "and why I'm declining the responsibility."

*

Michaels was looking over the charts. "All right, Owens, this wasn't the place I was heading for, but it will do. We're here and we've made an opening. Head for the crevice."

"Into the lungs?" said Owens, in outrage.

"No, no." Michaels bounded from his seat in impatience and climbed the stairs so that his head poked into the bubble. "We'll get into the pleural lining. Get the ship going and I'll guide you."

Cora knelt at Grant's chair. "How did you manage?"

Grant said, "Barely." Then, impatiently, he went on, "I kept thinking: why the devil am I here?"

Cora said, "Surely you know . . ."

Grant said, "No, I don't. The rest of you are driven by specific motivation, not by vague words. Owens is testing his ship; Michaels is piloting a course across a human body; Duval is admiring God's handiwork; and you . . ."

"Yes?"

Grant said softly, "You are admiring Duval."

Cora flushed. "He's worth admiration, he really is. You know, after he suggested we shine the ship's headlights into the crevice so as to give you something to shoot for, he did nothing further. He wouldn't say a word to you on your return. It's his way. He'll save someone's life, then be casually rude to him and what will be remembered will be his rudeness and not his life-saving. But his manner doesn't alter what he is."

"No. That's true; though it may mask it."

"Well, in any case, I've got to get to work on the laser." She cast a quick glance at Michaels, who was returning to his seat.

"The laser? Good lord, I'd forgotten. Well, then, do your best to see it's not crucially damaged, will you?"

The animation that had brightened her through the previous conversation died away. "Oh, if I only could."

She moved to the rear. Michaels' eyes followed her. "What about the laser?" he said.

Grant shook his head. "She's going to check now."

Michaels seemed to hesitate before his next remark. He shook his head slightly. Grant watched him but said nothing.

Michaels settled himself into his seat and said at last, "What do you think of our present situation?"

Grant, until now absorbed in Cora, looked up at the windows. They seemed to be moving between two walls that almost touched the *Proteus* on either side, gleaming yellow and constructed of parallel fibers, like huge tree trunks bound side by side.

The fluid about them was clear, free of cells and objects, almost free of debris. It seemed to be in dead calm and the *Proteus* churned through it at an even, rapid clip with only the muffled Brownian motion to interject any unevenness into its progress.

"The Brownian motion," said Grant, "is rougher now."

"The fluid here is less viscous than the blood plasma so the motion is less damped out. We won't be here long, however."

"We're not in the blood stream, I take it, then."

"Does it look like it? This is the space between the folds of the pleural membrane that lines the lungs. The membrane on that side is fixed to the ribs. In fact, we ought to be able to see a huge, gentle bulge when we pass one of them. The other membrane is fixed to the lungs. If you want the names, they are the parietal pleura and the pulmonary pleura, respectively."

"I don't really want the names."

"I didn't really think you did. What we're in now is a film of lubricating moisture between the pleurae. When the lungs expand during inhalation or contract during exhalation they move against the ribs and this fluid cushions and smooths the motion. There's so thin a film that the folds of the pleurae are commonly considered in contact in the healthy body, but, being germ-size, we can sneak between the folds through the film of fluid."

"When the lung wall moves along the rib cage, doesn't that affect us?"

"We are alternately hurried along slightly and held back slightly. Not enough to matter."

"Hey," said Grant. "Have these membranes anything to do with pleurisy?"

"They surely do. When the pleurae are infected and inflamed, every breath becomes an agony, and coughing . . ."

"What happens if Benes coughs?"

Michaels shrugged. "In our position now, I suppose it would be fatal. We'd come apart. There's no reason for coughing, however. He's under hypothermia and in deep sedation and his pleurae — take my word for it — are in good condition."

"But if we irritate them . . ."

"We're too small to do that."

"Are you sure?"

"We can speak only in terms of probabilities. The probability of a cough now is too small to worry about." His face was quite calm.

"I see," said Grant, and looked back to see what Cora was doing.

She and Duval were in the workroom, both heads bent closely over the bench. Grant rose and went to the doorway. Michaels joined him.

On a section of opal glass, illuminated from below into bright milkiness, the laser lay disassembled, each part etched sharp and clear against the light.

"What are the total damages now?" demanded Duval, crisply.

"Just those items, Doctor, and this broken trigger wire. That's all."

Thoughtfully, Duval seemed to be counting the parts, touching each with a delicate finger and moving it. "The key to the situation then is this smashed transistor. What it amounts to is that there's no way now to fire the lamp, and that's the end of the laser."

Grant interrupted. "Are there no spare parts?"

Cora looked up. Her glance drifted guiltily away from Grant's firm eyes. She said, "Not anything built into the chassis. We would have brought a second laser but who could have . . . if it hadn't come loose . . ."

Michaels said somberly, "Are you serious, Dr. Duval? Is the laser unusable?"

A note of impatience crept into Duval's voice. "I'm always serious. Now don't bother me." He seemed lost in thought.

Michaels shrugged. "That's it, then. We've gone through the heart, and we've filled our air chambers at the lungs, and all for nothing. We can't go on."

"Why not?" demanded Grant.

"Of course, we *can* go on as a matter of physical ability. It's just that there's no point in it, Grant. Without a laser, there's nothing we can do."

Grant said, "Dr. Duval, is there any way of performing the operation without the laser?"

"I'm thinking," snapped Duval.

"Then share your thoughts," snapped back Grant.

Duval looked up. "No, there's no way of performing the operation without the laser."

"But operations were performed for centuries without a laser. You cut through the lung wall with your knife; *that* was an operation. Can't you cut away the clot with your knife?"

"Of course I can, but not without damaging the nerve and placing an entire lobe of the brain in danger. The laser is incredibly more delicate than the knife. In this particular case, a knife would be butchery compared with a laser."

"But you can save Benes' life with the knife, can't you?"

"I think so, just maybe. I can't necessarily save his mind, however. In fact, I should think it almost certain that an operation with a knife would bring Benes through with serious mental deficiencies. Is that what you want?"

Grant rubbed his chin. "I'll tell you. We're heading for that clot. When we get there, if all we've got is a knife, you'll use a knife, Duval. If we lose our knives, you'll use your teeth, Duval. If you don't, I will. We may fail, but we won't quit. Meanwhile, let's look at the damn thing."

He pushed between Duval and Cora and picked up the transistor, which lay neatly on the tip of his first finger.

"Is this the broken one?"

"Yes," said Cora.

"If this were fixed or replaced, could you make the laser operate?"

"Yes, but there's no way of fixing it."

"Suppose you had another transistor about this size and power output and a thin enough wire. Could you piece it together?"

"I don't think I could. It requires such absolute precision."

"Perhaps you couldn't, but what about you, Dr. Duval? Your surgeon's fingers might be able to do it despite the Brownian motion."

"I could try, with Miss Peterson's help. But we don't have the parts."

Grant said, "Yes, we do. I can supply them."

He seized a heavy metal screwdriver and moved purposefully back into the front compartment. He went to his wireless and without hesitation began to unscrew the panel.

Michaels moved behind him, seizing his elbow. "What are you doing, Grant?"

Grant shook himself free. "I'm getting at its guts."

"You mean you're going to dismantle the wireless?"

"I need a transistor and a wire."

"But we'll be out of communication with the outside."

"So?"

"When the time comes to take us out of Benes . . . Grant, listen . . ."

Grant said, impatiently, "No. They can follow us through our radioactivity. The wireless is just for idle talk and we can do without. We have to, in fact. It's either radio silence or Benes' death."

"For God's sake, man, call Carter and put it to him."

Grant thought briefly. "I'll call him. But only to tell him there'll be no further messages."

"If he orders you to make ready for withdrawal . . ."

"I'll refuse."

"But if he *orders* you . . ."

"He can withdraw us by force, but without my cooperation. As long as we're aboard the *Proteus,* I make the policy decisions. We've gone through too much now to quit, so we go forward to the clot, whatever happens and whatever Carter orders."

*

Carter shouted, "Repeat last message."

"CANNIBALIZING WIRELESS TO REPAIR LASER. THIS LAST MESSAGE."

Reid said, blankly, "They're breaking communication."

Carter said, "What the devil happened to the laser?"

"Don't ask me."

Carter sat down heavily. "Have coffee brought up here, will you, Don? If I thought I could get away with it, I'd ask for a double scotch and soda, and then two more. We're *jinxed!*"

Reid had signaled for coffee. He said, "Sabotage, maybe."

"Sabotage?"

"Yes, and don't play innocent, General. You anticipated the possibility from the start, or why send Grant?"

"After what happened to Benes on the way here . . ."

"I know. And I don't particularly trust Duval or the girl, either."

"They're all right," said Carter, with a grimace. "They've got to be. Everyone here *has* to be right. There is no way to make security more secure."

"Exactly. No security procedure lends absolute certainty."

"All these people *work* here."

"Not Grant," said Reid.

"Eh?"

"Grant doesn't work here. He's an outsider."

Carter smiled contortedly. "He's a government agent."

Reid said, "I know. And agents can play double games. You put Grant on the *Proteus* and a string of bad luck begins — or what looks like bad luck —"

The coffee had come. Carter said, "That's ridiculous. I know the man. He's no stranger to me."

"When was the last time you saw him? What do you know about his inner life?"

"Forget it. It's impossible." But Carter stirred the cream into his coffee with a marked uneasiness.

Reid said, "All right. Just thinking out loud."

Carter said, "Are they still in the pleura?"

"Yes!"

Carter looked at the time-recorder, which said 32, and shook his head in frustration.

*

Grant had the wireless in fragments before him. Cora looked at the transistors one after the other, turning them, weighing them, seeming almost to peer within them.

"This one," she said, doubtfully, "will do, I think, but that wire is much too thick."

Duval placed the wire under question on the illuminated opal glass and placed the damaged fragment of original wire next to it, comparing them with somber eyes.

Grant said, "There's nothing closer. You'll have to make it do."

"It's easy to say that," said Cora. "You can give me an order like that, but you can't give such an order to the wire. It won't work no matter how hard you shout at it."

"All right. All right." Grant tried to think, and got nowhere.

Duval said, "Now wait. With luck, I may be able to scrape it thin enough. Miss Peterson, get me a number eleven scalpel."

He placed the wire from what had been Grant's device (now wireless in literal truth) in two small clamps and swung a magnifying glass before it. He reached out for the scalpel which Cora placed within his grip and slowly, he began to scrape.

Without looking up, he said, "Kindly take your seat, Grant. You cannot help me by snorting over my shoulder."

Grant flinched a little, caught Cora's look of appeal. He said nothing and moved back to his seat.

Michaels, in his seat, greeted him humorlessly. "The surgeon is at work," he said. "The scalpel is in his hand and his temperament is at once at its full bent. Don't waste your time being angry with him."

Grant said, "I'm not angry with him."

Michaels said, "Of course you are, unless you're prepared to tell me you've resigned from the human race. Duval has the gift — the God-given gift, I'm sure he would say — of antagonizing people with a single word, a glance, a gesture. And if that weren't enough, there is the young lady."

Grant turned to Michaels with clear impatience. "What about the young lady?"

"Come now, Grant. Do you want a lecture on boys and girls?"

Grant frowned and turned away.

Michaels said softly, rather sadly, "You're in a quandary about her, aren't you?"

"What quandary?"

"She's a nice girl; *very* good-looking. And yet you're a professionally suspicious person."

"Well?"

"Well! What happened to the laser? Was it an accident?"

"It could have been."

"Yes, it could have been." Michaels' voice was a bare whisper. "But was it?"

Grant whispered, too, after a quick glance over his shoulder. "Are you accusing Miss Peterson of sabotaging the mission?"

"I? Of course not. I have no evidence of that. But I suspect *you* are accusing her in your mind and you don't like to be doing so. Hence the quandary."

"Why Miss Peterson?"

"Why not? Nobody would pay any attention to her if she were seen fiddling with the laser. It is her province. And if she were intent on sabotage, she would naturally gravitate to that part of the mission with which she felt most at home — the laser."

"Which would place immediate and automatic suspicion upon her — as it seems to have done," said Grant, with some heat.

"I see. You are angry."

Grant said, "Look. We're all in one relatively small ship and you might think that we were each of us under the close and constant observation of the others, but that's not so. We've been so absorbed with what's out there, all of us, that any one of us could have walked back to the storage compartment and done anything he wanted to the laser and done so unnoticed. You or I might have done it. I wouldn't have seen you. You wouldn't have seen me."

"Or Duval?"

"Or Duval. I'm not eliminating him. Or it might have been an honest accident."

"And your lifeline coming loose? Another accident?"

"Are you prepared to suggest anything else?"

"No, I'm not. I can point out a few things, if you're in the mood."

"I'm not, but point them out anyway."

"It was Duval who secured your lifeline."

"And apparently made a poor knot, I suppose," said Grant. "Still there was considerable tension on the line. Considerable."

"A surgeon should be able to tie knots."

"That's nonsense. Surgical knots are not sailors' knots."

"Perhaps. On the other hand, maybe the knot was deliberately tied so as to come loose. Or perhaps it could have been untied by hand."

Grant nodded. "All right. But there again, everyone had their attention on what was going on about them. You, or Duval, or Miss Peterson, might have moved quickly back to the ship, loosened the knot, and returned without being noticed. Even Owens might have left the ship for the purpose, I suppose."

"Yes, but Duval had the best chance. Just before you broke loose, he went back to the ship, carrying the snorkel. He said the lifeline came loose as he watched. We know by his own admission that he was in the right place at the right time."

"And it might still have been an accident. What's his motive? The laser had already been sabotaged, and all he could accomplish by loosening the lifeline would be to endanger me personally. If he was after the mission, why bother with me?"

"Oh, Grant! Oh, Grant!" Michaels smiled and shook his head.

"Well, talk. Don't just grunt."

"Suppose it was the young lady who took care of the laser. And suppose Duval's interest was specifically you; suppose he wanted to get rid of you, with damage to the mission strictly secondary."

Grant stared speechlessly.

Michaels went on. "Duval is perhaps not so entirely devoted to his work that he doesn't notice his assistant seems aware of your existence. You are a fine-looking young man, Grant, and you had saved her serious injury at the time of the whirlpool; perhaps even her life. Duval watched that and he must have watched her reaction."

"There was no reaction. She's not interested in me."

"I watched her when you were lost in the alveolus. She was distraught. What was obvious to anyone then might have been obvious to Duval much sooner — that she was attracted to you. And he might have gotten rid of you for that reason."

Grant bit at his lower lip in thought, then said, "All right. And the loss of air? Was that an accident, too?"

Michaels shrugged. "I don't know. I suspect you will suggest that Owens might have been responsible for that."

"He might. He knows the ship. He designed it. He can best gimmick its controls. And only he checked on what was wrong."

"That's right, you know. That's right."

"And for that matter," went on Grant with gathering anger, "what about the arterio-venous fistula? Was that an accident, or did you know it was there?"

Michaels sat back in his chair and looked blank. "Good lord, I hadn't thought of that. I give you my word, Grant, I sat here and honestly thought there wasn't a thing that happened that could possibly point in my direction specifically. I realized that it could be maintained that I had slyly damaged the laser or undone your lifeline knot or jammed the air chamber valve when no one was looking — or all three, for that matter. But in each case it was so much more likely that someone else had done it. The fistula, I admit, could be no one but myself."

"That's right."

"Except, of course, that I didn't know it was there. But I can't prove that, can I?"

"No."

Michaels said, "Do you ever read detective stories, Grant?"

"In my younger days I read quite a few. Now . . ."

"Your profession spoils the fun. Yes, I can well imagine that. But you know, in detective stories, it is always so simple. A subtle clue points to one person and one person only and the detective sees it though no one else does. In real life, it seems, the clues point everywhere."

"Or nowhere," said Grant, firmly. "We could be dealing with a series of accidents and misfortunes."

"We could," conceded Michaels.

Neither, however, sounded very convincing. Or convinced.

CHAPTER 14 LYMPHATIC

OWENS' VOICE sounded from the bubble, "Dr. Michaels, look ahead. Is that the turnoff?"

They could feel the *Proteus* slowing.

Michaels muttered, "Too much talk. I should have been watching."

Immediately ahead was an open-ended tube. The thin walls facing them were ragged, almost fading away into nothingness. The opening was barely wide enough for the *Proteus.*

"Good enough," called out Michaels. "Head into it."

Cora had left the workbench to look forward in wonder, but Duval remained in his place, still working, with infinite, untiring patience.

"That must be a lymphatic," she said.

They had entered and the walls surrounded them, no thicker than those of the capillary they had left some time back.

As in the capillaries, the walls were made up, quite clearly, of cells in the shape of flat polygons, each with a rounded nucleus at the center. The fluid through which they were passing was very similar to that in the pleural cavity, sparkling yellowish in the *Proteus* headlights, and lending a yellow cast to the cells. The nuclei were deeper in color, almost orange.

Grant said, "Poached eggs! They look exactly like poached eggs!" Then, "What's a lymphatic?"

"It's an auxiliary circulatory system in a way," said Cora, explaining eagerly. "Fluid squeezes out of the very thin capillaries and collects in spaces in the body and between the cells. That's interstitial fluid. These drain off into tiny tubes, or lymphatics, that are open at their ends, as you saw just now. These tubes gradually combine into larger and larger tubes until the largest are the size of veins. All the lymph . . ."

"That's the fluid about us?" asked Grant.

"Yes. All the lymph is collected into the largest lymphatic of all, the thoracic duct, which leads into the subclavian vein in the upper chest, and thus the lymph is restored to the main circulatory system."

"And why have we entered the lymphatic?"

Michaels leaned back, the course momentarily secure. "Well," he put in, "it's a quiet backwater. There's no pumping effect of the heart. Muscular pressures and tensions move the fluid and Benes isn't having many of those right now. So we can be assured a quiet journey to the brain."

"Why didn't we enter the lumphatics to begin with, then?"

"They are small. An artery is a much better target for a hypodermic; and the arterial current was expected to carry us to target in minutes. It didn't work out and to make our way back into an artery from here would delay us badly. Then, once we reached the artery, we would receive a battering which the ship might no longer be able to take."

He spread out a new set of charts and called out, "Owens, are you following Chart 72-D?"

"Yes, Dr. Michaels."

"Make sure you follow the path I've traced. It will take us through a minimum number of nodes."

Grant said, "What's that up ahead?"

Michaels looked up and froze. "Slow the ship," he cried.

The *Proteus* decelerated vigorously. Through one portion of the wall of the widening tube a shapeless mass protruded, milky, granular, and somehow threatening. But as they watched, it shrank and vanished.

"Move on," said Michaels. He said to Grant, "I was afraid that white cell might be coming, but it was going, fortunately. Some of the white cells are formed in the lymph nodes, which are an important barrier against disease. They form not only white cells but also antibodies."

"And what are antibodies?"

"Protein molecules that have the capacity to combine specifically with various outside substances invading the body; germs, toxins, foreign proteins."

"And us?"

"And us, I suppose, under proper circumstances."

Cora interposed. "Bacteria are trapped in the nodes, which serve as a battleground between them and the white cells. The nodes swell up and become painful. You know, children get what are called swollen glands in the armpits or at the angle of the jaw."

"And they're really swollen lymph nodes."

"That's right."

Grant said, "It sounds like a good idea to stay away from the lymph nodes."

Michaels said, "We are small. Benes' antibody system is not sensitized to us, and there is only one series of nodes we need pass through, after which we have clear sailing. It's a chance, of course, but everything we do now is a chance. Or," he demanded, challengingly, "are you going to set policy by ordering me out of the lymphatic system?"

Grant shook his head, "No. Not unless someone suggests a better alternative."

*

"There it is," said Michaels, nudging Grant gently. "See it?"

"The shadow up ahead?"

"Yes. This lymphatic is one of several that enters the node, which is a spongy mass of membranes and tortuous passages. The place is full of lymphocytes . . ."

"What are those?"

"One of the types of white cells. They won't bother us, I hope. Any bacteria in the circulatory system reaches a lymph node eventually. It can't negotiate the narrow twisting channels . . ."

"Can we?"

"We move deliberately, Grant, and with an end in view, whereas bacteria drift blindly. You do see the difference, I hope. Once trapped in the node, the bacterium is handled by antibodies or, if that fails, by white cells mobilized for battle."

The shadow was close now. The golden tinge of the lymph was darkening and turning cloudy. Up ahead there seemed a wall.

"Do you have the course, Owens?" Michaels called out.

"I have, but it's going to be easy to make a wrong turning."

"Even if you do, remember that at this moment we are heading generally upward. Keep the gravitometer indicator on the line as steadily as you can, and in the end you can't go wrong."

The *Proteus* made a sharp turn and suddenly all was gray. The headlights seemed to pick up nothing that was not a shadow of a deeper or lighter gray. There was an occasional small rod, shorter than the ship and much narrower; clumps of spherical objects, quite small, and with fuzzy boundaries.

"Bacteria," muttered Michaels. "I see them in too great detail to recognize the exact species. Isn't that strange? Too much detail."

The *Proteus* was moving more slowly now, following the many gentle sweeps and turns of the channel almost hesitantly.

Duval stepped to the door of the workroom. "What's going on? I can't work on this thing if the ship doesn't hold a steady course. The Brownian motion is bad enough."

"Sorry, Doctor," said Michaels, coldly. "We're passing through a lymph node and this is the best we can do."

Duval, looking angry, turned away.

Grant peered forward. "It's getting messy up there, Dr. Michaels. What is that stuff that looks like seaweed or something?"

"Reticular fibers," said Michaels.

Owens said, "Dr. Michaels."

"Yes?"

"That fibrous stuff is getting thicker. I won't be able to maneuver through them without doing some damage to them."

Michaels looked thoughtful. "Don't worry about that. Any damage we do will, in any case, be minimal."

A clump of fibers pulled loose as the *Proteus* nudged into it, slipped and slid along the window and vanished past the sides. It happened again and again with increasing frequency.

"It's all right, Owens," said Michaels, encouragingly, "the body can repair damage like this without trouble."

"I'm not worried about Benes," called out Owens. "I'm worried about the ship. If this stuff clogs the vents, the engine will overheat. And it's adhering to us. Can't you tell the difference in the engine sound?"

Grant couldn't, and his attention turned to the outside again. The ship was nosing through a forest of tendrils now. They glinted a kind of menacing maroon in the headlights.

"We'll get through it soon," said Michaels, but there was a definite note of anxiety in his voice.

The way did clear a bit and now Grant could indeed sense a difference in the sound of the engines, almost a thickening hoarseness, as though the clear echo of gases bubbling through exhaust vents was being muffled and choked off.

Owens shouted, "Dead ahead!"

There was a soggy collision of a bacterial rod with the ship. The substance of the bacterium bent about the curve of the window, sprang back into shape and bounced off, leaving a smear that washed off slowly.

There were others ahead.

"What's going on?" said Grant in wonder.

"I think," said Michaels, "I *think* we're witnessing antibody reaction to bacteria. White cells aren't involved. See! Watch the walls of the bacteria. It's hard by the reflection of miniaturized light, but can you see it?"

"No, I'm afraid I can't."

Duval's voice sounded behind them. "I can't see anything, either."

Grant turned. "Is the wire adjusted, Doctor?"

"Not yet," said Duval. "I can't work in this mess. It will have to wait. What's this about antibodies?"

Michaels said, "As long as you're not working, let's have the inner lights out. Owens!"

The lights went out and the only illumination came from without, a ghostly gray-maroon flicker that placed all their faces in angry shadow.

"What's going on outside?" asked Cora.

"That's what I'm trying to explain," said Michaels. "Watch the edges of the bacteria ahead."

Grant did his best, narrowing his eyes. The light was unsteady and flickering. "You mean those small objects that look like BB shot."

"Exactly. They're antibody molecules. Proteins, you know,

and large enough to see on our scale. There's one nearby. See it!"

One of the small antibodies had swirled past the window. At close quarters it did not seem to be a BB shot at all. It seemed rather larger than a BB and to be a tiny tangle of spaghetti, vaguely spherical. Thin strands, visible only as fine glints of light, protruded here and there.

"What are they doing?" asked Grant.

"Each bacterium has a distinctive cell wall made out of specific atomic groupings hooked up in a specific way. To us, the various walls look smooth and featureless; but if we were smaller still — on the molecular scale instead of the bacterial — we'd see that each wall had a mosaic pattern, and that this mosaic was different and distinctive in each bacterial species. The antibodies can fit neatly upon this mosaic and once they cover key portions of the wall, the bacterial cell is through; it would be like blocking a man's nose and mouth and choking him to death."

Cora said excitedly, "You can see them cluster. How . . . how horrible."

"Are you sorry for the bacteria, Cora?" said Michaels, smiling.

"No, but the antibodies seem so vicious, the way they pounce."

Michaels said, "Don't give them human emotions. They are only molecules, moving blindly. Inter-atomic forces pull them against those portions of the wall which they fit and hold them there. It's analogous to the clank of a magnet against an iron bar. Would you say the magnet attacks the iron viciously?"

Knowing what to look for, Grant could now see what was happening. A bacterium, moving blindly through a cloud of hovering antibodies seemed to attract them, to pull them in to itself. In moments. its wall had grown fuzzy with them. The antibodies lined up side by side, their spaghetti projections entangling.

Grant said, "Some of the antibodies seem indifferent. They don't touch the bacterium."

"The antibodies are specific," said Michaels. "Each one is designed to fit the mosaic of a particular kind of bacterium, or of a particular protein molecule. Right now, most of the antibodies, though not all, fit the bacteria surrounding us. The presence of these particular bacteria has stimulated the rapid formation of this particular variety of antibody. How this stimulation is brought about, we still don't know."

"Good lord," cried Duval. "Look at that."

One of the bacteria was now solidly encased in antibodies which had followed its every irregularity, so that it seemed to be exactly as before, but with a fuzzy, thickened boundary.

Cora said, "It fits perfectly."

"No, not that. Don't you see that the intermolecular bindings of the antibody molecules produce a kind of pressure on the bacterium? This was never clear even in electron microscopy, which only shows us dead objects."

A silence fell upon the crew of the *Proteus*, which was now moving slowly past the bacterium. The antibody coating seemed to stiffen and tighten and the bacterium within writhed. The coating stiffened and tightened again, then again, and suddenly the bacterium seemed to crumple and give way. The antibodies drew together and what had been a rod became a featureless ovoid.

"They killed the bacterium. They literally squeezed it to death," said Cora, with revulsion.

"Remarkable," muttered Duval. "What a weapon for research we have in the *Proteus*."

Grant said, "Are you sure we're safe from the antibodies?"

Michaels said, "It seems so. We're not the sort of thing for which antibodies are designed."

"Are you sure? I have a feeling they can be designed for any shape, if properly stimulated."

"You're right, I suppose. Still, we're obviously not stimulating them."

Owens called out, "More fibers ahead, Dr. Michaels. We're pretty well coated with the stuff. It's cutting down our speed."

Michaels said, "We're almost out of the node, Owens."

Occasionally a writhing bacterium slammed against the ship, which shuddered in response, but the fight was thinning out now, the bacteria clearly the losers. The *Proteus* was bumping and nudging its way through fibers again.

"Right ahead," said Michaels. "One more left turn and we're at the efferent lymphatic."

Owens said, "We're trailing the fibers. The *Proteus* looks like a shaggy dog."

Grant said, "How many more lymph nodes on the course to the brain?"

"Three more. One may be avoidable. I'm not quite sure."

"We can't do that. We lose too much time. We won't make it through three more like this. Are there any—any short cuts?"

Michaels shook his head. "None that won't create problems worse than those we now face. Sure, we'll make it through the nodes. The fibers will wash off, and if we don't stop to look at bacterial warfare, we can go faster."

"And next time," said Grant, frowning, "we'll meet a fight involving white cells."

Duval stepped over to Michaels' charts and said, "Where are we now, Michaels?"

"Right here," said Michaels, watching the surgeon narrowly.

Duval thought a moment and said, "Let me get my bearings. We're in the neck now, aren't we?"

"Yes."

Grant thought: In the neck? Right where they had started. He looked at the time-recorder. It said 28. More than half the time gone and they were back where they had started.

Duval said, "Can't we avoid all nodes, and actually take a short cut, too, if we turn off somewhere around here and make straight for the inner ear? From that to the clot is no distance at all."

Michaels wrinkled his forehead into a washboard and sighed. "On the map that looks fine. You make a quick mark on the chart and you're home safe. But have you thought what passing through the inner ear means?"

Duval said, "No. What?"

"The ear, my dear Doctor, as I needn't tell you, is a device for concentrating and amplifying sound waves. The slightest sound, the *slightest* sound outside, will set up intense vibrations in the inner ear. On our miniaturized scale those vibrations will be deadly."

Duval looked thoughtful. "Yes, I see."

Grant said, "Is the inner ear *always* vibrating?"

"Unless there's silence, with no sound above the hearing threshold. Even then, on our scale, we'll probably detect some gentle motions."

"Worse than Brownian motion?"

"Perhaps not."

Grant said, "The sound has to come from outside, doesn't it? If we pass through the inner ear, the throbbing of the ship's engine or the sound of our voices won't affect it, will it?"

"No, I'm sure it won't. The inner ear isn't designed for our miniaturized vibrations."

"Well, then, if the people out there in the hospital room maintain complete silence . . ."

"How will we get them to do so?" demanded Michaels. Then, almost brutally, "*You* demolished the wireless so we can't get in touch with them."

"But they can track us. They'll find us heading for the inner ear. They'll understand the need for silence."

"Will they?"

"Won't they?" said Grant, impatiently. "Most of them there are medical men. They have an understanding of such matters."

"Do you want to take that kind of chance?"

Grant looked about. "What do the rest of you think?"

Owens said, "I'll follow any course that's set for me, but I'm not going to set it for myself."

Duval said, "I'm not sure."

Michaels said, "And I *am* sure. I'm against it."

Grant looked briefly at Cora, who sat in silence.

"All right," he said. "The responsibility is mine. We're heading for the inner ear. Set the course, Michaels."

Michaels said, "Look here . . ."

"The decision is made, Michaels. Set the course."

Michaels flushed and then shrugged. "Owens," he said, coldly. "We'll have to make a sharp left turn at the point I am now indicating . . ."

CHAPTER 15 EAR

CARTER lifted his coffee cup absently. Drops of liquid slipped off and landed on his pants leg. He noticed that but paid it no attention. "What do you mean, they've veered off?"

"I should guess they felt they had spent too much time in the lymph node and didn't want to go through any more of them," said Reid.

"All right. Where are they going instead?"

"I'm not positive yet, but they seem to be headed for the inner ear. I'm not sure that I approve of that."

Carter put down his cup again and shoved it to one side. He had not placed it to his lips. "Why not?" He glanced quickly at the time-recorder. It read 27.

"It will be difficult. We'll have to watch out for sound."

"Why?"

"You can figure it out, can't you, Al? The ear reacts to sound. The cochlea vibrates. If the *Proteus* is anywhere near it, it will vibrate, too, and it may vibrate to destruction."

Carter leaned forward in his seat, staring at Reid's calm face. "Why the hell are they going there, then?"

"I suppose because they think that's the only route that will get them to destination fast enough. Or, on the other hand, they may just be crazy. We have no way of telling since they cannibalized their wireless."

Carter said, "Are they in there yet? In the inner ear, I mean?"

Reid flicked a switch and asked a quick question. He turned back. "Just about."

"Do the men down there in the operating room understand about the necessity for silence?"

"I suppose so."

"You *suppose* so. What good is supposing?"

"They won't be in it long."

"They'll be in it long enough. Listen, you tell those men down there . . . no, too late to take a chance. Get me a piece of paper and call in someone from outside. Anyone. Anyone."

An armed security man came in and saluted.

"Oh, shut up," said Carter, wearily. He didn't return the salute. He had scribbled on the paper in block letters: SILENCE! ABSOLUTE SILENCE WHILE PROTEUS IS IN EAR.

"Take this," he said to the security man. "You go down into the operating room and show it to each man. Make sure he looks at it. If you make any noise I'll kill you. If you say one word, I'll disembowel you first. Do you understand?"

"Yes, sir," he said, but looked confused and alarmed.

"Go ahead. Hurry. Damn it, take off your shoes."

"Sir?"

"Take them off. You walk into that room on stocking feet."

They watched from the observation room, counting the interminable seconds until the stockinged soldier walked into the operating room. From doctor to nurse to doctor he went, holding up the paper and jerking a thumb up toward the control room. Person after person nodded grimly. None budged from his or her spot. For a moment, it seemed a mass paralysis had gripped everyone in the room.

"Obviously they understand," said Reid. "Even without instructions."

"I congratulate them," said Carter, savagely. "Now, listen, you get in touch with the various guys at controls. No buzzers must sound, no bells, no gongs, nothing. For that matter, no flashing lights. I don't want anyone to be startled into as much as a grunt."

"They'll be through in a few seconds."

"Maybe," said Carter, "and maybe not. Hop to it."

Reid hopped to it.

*

The *Proteus* had entered a wide region of pure liquid. Except for a few antibodies flashing by, now and then, there was nothing to be seen except the glitter of the ship's headlights making its way through the yellow-tinged lymph.

A dim sound below the threshold of hearing rubbed over the ship, almost as though it had slid against a washboard. Then again. And again.

Michaels called out, "Owens, put out the cabin lights, will you?"

The exterior leaped into greater clarity at once. "Do you see that?" Michaels asked.

The others stared. Grant saw nothing at all.

"We're in the cochlear duct," said Michaels. "Inside the little spiral tube in the inner ear that does our hearing for us. This one does Benes' hearing for him. It vibrates to sound in different patterns. See?"

Now Grant saw. It was almost like a shadow in the fluid, a huge, flat shadow whipping past them.

"It's a sound wave," said Michaels. "At least, in a manner of speaking. A wave of compression which we somehow make out with our miniaturized light."

"Does that mean someone is talking?" asked Cora.

"Oh, no. If someone were talking or making any real sound, this thing would heave like the granddaddy of all earthquakes. Even in absolute silence, though, the cochlea picks up sounds; the distant thud of the heartbeat, the rasp of blood working through the tiny veins and arteries of the ear, and so on. Didn't you ever cup your ear with a shell and listen to the sound of the ocean? What you're listening to mainly is the magnified sound of your own ocean, the blood stream."

Grant said, "Will this be dangerous?"

Michaels shrugged. "No worse than it is — if no one talks."

Duval, back in the workroom, and bent over the laser once more, said, "Why are we slowing? Owens!"

Owens said, "Something's wrong. The engine is choking off and I don't know why."

There was the slowly intensifying sensation of being in a down-dropping elevator as the *Proteus* settled lower in the duct.

They hit bottom with a slight jar and Duval put down his scalpel. "Now what?"

Owens said anxiously, "The engine is overheating and I had to stop it. I think . . ."

"What?"

"It must be those reticular fibers. The damned seaweed. It must have blocked the intake vents. There's nothing else I can think of that would be causing this."

"Can you blow them out?" asked Grant, tensely.

Owens shook his head. "Not a chance. Those are intake vents. They suck inward."

"Well, then, there's only one thing to do," said Grant. "It has to be cleaned off from the outside and that means more skin-diving." With furrowed brow, he began to clamber into his diving outfit.

Cora was looking anxiously out the window.

She said, "There are antibodies out there."

"Not many," said Grant, briefly.

"But what if they attack?"

"Not likely," said Michaels, reassuringly. "They're not sensitized to the human shape. And as long as no damage is done to the tissues themselves, the antibodies probably will remain passive."

"See," said Grant, but Cora shook her head.

Duval, who had listened for a moment, bent down to look at the wire he was shaving, matching it against the original wire thoughtfully, and then turning it in his hands slowly to try to gauge the evenness of its cross-section.

Grant dropped out the ventral hatch of the ship, landing on the soft rubber elasticity of the lower wall of the cochlear duct. He looked ruefully at the ship. It was not the clean, smooth metal it had been. It looked furry, shaggy.

He kicked off into the lymph, propelling himself toward the bow of the ship. Owens was quite correct. The intake valves were choked with the fibers.

Grant seized a double handful and pulled. They came loose with difficulty, many breaking off at the surface of the vent filters.

Michaels' voice reached him over his small receiver. "How is it?"

"Pretty damn rotten," said Grant.

"How long will it take you? We've got a 26 reading on the time-recorder."

"It's going to take me quite a while." Grant yanked desperately, but the viscosity of the lymph slowed his movements and the tenacity of the fibers seemed to fight back.

Within the ship, Cora said, tensely, "Wouldn't it be better if some of us went out to help him?"

"Well, now," began Michaels, doubtfully.

"*I'm* going to." She seized her suit.

Michaels said, "All right. I will, too. Owens had better stay at the controls."

Duval said, "And I think I had better stay right here, too. I have this thing almost done."

"Of course, Dr. Duval," said Cora. She adjusted her swimming mask.

The task was scarcely eased by the fact that three of them were soon wiggling about the ship's bow, all three snatching desperately at the fibers, pulling them loose, letting them drift away in the slow current. The metal of the filters was beginning to show and Grant pushed some recalcitrant pieces into the vent.

"I hope this doesn't do any harm, but I *can't* get them out. Owens, what if some of these fibers get into the vents; inside, I mean?"

Owens' voice in his ear said, "Then they get carbonized in the motor and foul it. It will mean a nasty cleaning job when we're through."

"Once we get through, I don't care if you have to scrap this stinking ship." Grant pushed at the fibers that were flush with the filters and pulled at those that weren't. Cora and Michaels did the same.

Cora said, "We're making it."

Michaels said, "But we're in the cochlea a lot longer than we had expected to be. At any moment, some sound . . ."

"Shut up," said Grant irritably, "and finish the job."

*

Carter made as if to tear at his hair and then held back. "No, no, no, NO!" he cried. "They've stopped again."

He pointed at the message written on a piece of paper and held up in his direction from one of the television screens.

"At least he remembered not to talk," said Reid. "Why do you suppose they've stopped?"

"How in blue blazing damnation do I know? Maybe they've stopped for a coffee-break. Maybe they've decided to stop for a sun bath. Maybe the girl . . ."

He broke off. "Well, I don't know. All I do know is that we have only twenty-four minutes left."

Reid said, "The longer they stay in the inner ear, the more nearly certain it will be that some joker will make a sound . . . sneeze . . . something."

"You're right." Carter thought, then said softly, "Oh, for the love of Mike. It's the simple solutions we don't see. Call in that messenger boy."

The security man entered again. He didn't salute.

Carter said, "You still have your shoes off? Okay. Take this down and show it to one of the nurses. You remember about the disemboweling?"

"Yes, sir."

The message read: COTTON AT BENES' EARS.

Carter lit a cigar and watched through the control window as the security man entered, hesitated a moment, then moved with quick, gingerly steps to one of the nurses.

She smiled, looked up at Carter and made a circle of her thumb and forefinger.

Carter said, "I have to think of everything."

Reid said, "It will just deaden the noise. It won't stop it."

"You know what they say about half a loaf," said Carter.

The nurse slipped off her own shoes and was at one of the tables in two steps. Carefully, she opened a fresh box of absorbent cotton and unrolled two feet of it.

She pulled off a fistful in one hand, and seized a fistful in the other. It didn't come readily. She pulled harder. Her hand went flying outward, striking a pair of scissors on the table.

It skittered off the table, striking the hard floor. The nurse's foot flew desperately after it, clamping down upon it hard, but not until after it had given out one sharp, metallic clang like the hiccup of a fallen angel.

The nurse's face reddened into a look of deathly horror; everyone else in the room turned to stare, and Carter, dropping his cigar, crumpled into his chair.

"Finished!" he said.

*

Owens turned on the engine and gently checked the controls. The needle on the temperature gauge, which had been well into the danger zone almost since they had entered the cochlear duct, was dropping.

He said, "It looks good. Are you all set out there?"

Grant's voice sounded in his ear. "Nothing much left. Get ready to move. We're coming in."

And at that moment, the universe seemed to heave. It was as though a fist had driven up against the *Proteus*, which lifted high. Owens seized a panel for support and held on desperately, listening to a distant thunder.

Below, Duval, as desperately, held on to the laser, trying to cushion it against a world gone mad.

Outside, Grant felt himself flung high in the air as though caught in the grip of a huge tidal wave. He flipped over and over and plunged into the wall of the cochlear duct. He was shaken loose from the wall, which seemed to be caving forward.

Somewhere in a miraculously calm segment of his mind, Grant knew that on the ordinary scale the wall was responding with rapid vibrations of microscopic amplitude to some sharp sound, but that thought was buried in sheer shock.

Grant tried desperately to locate the *Proteus* but he caught only a quick glimpse of its headlights flashing against a distant section of the wall.

Cora had been holding on to a projection of the *Proteus* at the moment the vibration had struck. Instinctively, her grip tightened and for a moment she rode the *Proteus* as though it were an insanely bucking bronco. The breath was jerked out of her and, when her grip was torn away, she went skidding across the floor of the membrane on which the ship had been resting.

The ship's headlights caught the path ahead of her and though she tried in horror to brake her motion it was quite useless. She might as well have tried to dig her heels into the ground in order to stop an avalanche.

She was heading, she knew, for a section of the organ of Corti, the basic center of hearing. Included among the components of the organ were the hair cells; fifteen thousand of them altogether. She could make out a few of them now; each with its delicate, microscopic cilium held high. Certain numbers of them vibrated gently according to the pitch and intensity of the sound waves conducted into the inner ear and there amplified.

That, however, was as she might have considered it in some course in physiology; phrases as they might have been used in the universe of normal scale. Here, what she saw was a sheer precipice and beyond it a series of tall, graceful columns, moving in stately fashion, not all in unison, but rather first one and then another as though a swaying wave were rippling over the entire structure.

Cora went skidding and spinning over the precipice into a world of vibrating columns and walls. Her headlight flashed erratically as she went tumbling downward. She felt the pull of something on her harness and swung forcefully against a firmly elastic object. She dangled head downward, afraid to struggle lest whatever projection had stopped her would give way and let her fall the rest of the way.

She spun first this way, then that, as the column against which she clung, a microscopic cilium on one hair cell of the organ of Corti, continued to sway majestically.

She was managing to breathe now and heard her own name. Someone was calling. Carefully, she made a pleading sound. Encouraged by the sound of her voice, she screamed as shrilly as she could, "Help! Everybody! Help!"

*

The first devastating shock had passed and Owens was bringing the *Proteus* under control in a still-turbulent sea. The sound, whatever it was, might have been intense but it had been sharp and quick dying. That alone saved them. Had it continued for even a short time . . .

Duval, cradling the laser under one arm and seated with his back against the wall and his legs pressing desperately against a bench support, shouted, "All clear?"

"I think we pulled through," gasped Owens. "The controls respond."

"We had better leave."

"We've got to pick up the others."

Duval said, "Oh, yes. I had forgotten." Carefully, he rolled over, got one hand beneath to steady himself and then slowly made it to his feet. He still clutched the laser. "Get them in."

Owens called, "Michaels! Grant! Miss Peterson!"

"Coming in," responded Michaels. "I *think* I'm in one piece."

"Wait," called Grant. "I don't see Cora."

The *Proteus* was steady now and Grant, breathing heavily, and feeling more than a little shaken, was swimming strongly toward its headlight.

He called, "Cora!"

She answered shrilly, "Help! Everybody! Help!"

Grant looked about in every direction. He shouted, desperately, "Cora! Where are you?"

Her voice in his ear said, "I can't tell you exactly. I'm caught among the hair cells."

"Where are they? Michaels, where are the hair cells?"

Grant could make out Michaels approaching the ship from another direction, his body a dim shadow in the lymph, his small headlight cutting a thin swath ahead of him.

Michaels said, "Wait, let me get my bearings." He flipped quickly, then shouted, "Owens, turn on ship's headlight wide-angle."

Light spread in response and Michaels said, "This way! Owens, follow me! We'll need the light."

Grant followed Michaels' quickly-moving figure and saw the precipice and columns ahead.

"In there?" he asked uncertainly.

"Must be," returned Michaels.

They were at the edge now, with the ship behind them and its headlight spilling into the cavernous file of columns, still swaying gently.

"I don't see her," said Michaels.

"I do," said Grant, pointing. "Isn't that she? Cora! I see you. Move your arm so I can be certain."

She waved.

"All right. I'm coming to get you. We'll have you back in a shake and a half."

Cora waited and felt a touch at her knee, the faintest and gentlest sensation, like that of a fly's wing brushing against her. She looked toward her knee but saw nothing.

There was another touch near her shoulder, then still another.

Quite suddenly, she made them out, just a few—the little balls of wool, with their quivering out-thrusting filaments. The protein molecules of the antibodies. It was almost as though they were exploring her surface, testing her, *tasting* her, deciding whether she were harmless or not. There were only a few, but more were drifting toward her from among the columns. With the headlights from the *Proteus* shining down, she could make them out clearly, in the glittering reflection of miniaturized light. Each filament shone like a questing sunbeam.

She screamed, "Come quickly. There are antibodies all about." In her thoughts she could see, all too clearly, the antibodies coating the bacterial cell, fuzzing it completely, then crushing it as intermolecular forces drew the antibodies together.

An antibody had touched her elbow and was clinging there. She shook her arm in revulsion and horror, so that her whole body writhed and went slamming into the column. The antibody did not shake loose. Another joined it, the two fitting together neatly, filaments interlaced.

*

"Antibodies," muttered Grant.

Michaels said, "She must have done enough damage to surrounding tissue to spark their appearance."

"Can they do anything to her?"

"Not immediately. They're not sensitized to her. No antibodies are deliberately designed for her form. But some will fit somewhere on a sheerly random basis and she will stimulate the formation of more like those that do fit. Then they'll come swarming."

Grant could see them now, swarming already, settling about her like a cloud of tiny fruit flies.

He said, "Michaels, get back to the sub. One person is enough to risk. I'll get her out of here somehow. If I don't, it will be up to the three of you to get whatever's left of us back into the ship. We can't be allowed to deminiaturize here, whatever happens."

Michaels hesitated, then said, "Take care," and turned, hastening back to the *Proteus*.

Grant continued to plunge toward Cora. The turbulence caused by his approach sent the antibodies spinning and dancing rapidly.

"Let's get you out of here, Cora," he panted.

"Oh, Grant. Quickly."

He was pulling desperately at her oxygen cylinders, which had cut into a column and stuck. Thick strands of viscous material were still oozing outward from the break and it was that, perhaps, which had triggered the arrival of the antibodies.

"Don't move, Cora. Let me . . . ah!" Cora's ankle was caught between two fibers and he strained them apart. "Now, come with me."

Both executed a half-somersault and started moving away. Cora's body was fuzzed with clinging antibodies but the bulk were left behind. Then, following who knew what kind of equivalent of scent on the microscopic scale, they began to follow; first a few, then many, then the entire growing swarm.

"We'll never make it," gasped Cora.

"Yes, we will," said Grant. "Just put every muscle you have into it."

"But they're still attaching themselves. I'm scared, Grant."

Grant looked over his shoulder at her, then fell back slightly. Her back was half-covered by a mosaic of the wool-balls. They had gauged the nature of her surface well, that part of it at least.

He brushed her back hurriedly, but the antibodies clung, flattening out at the touch of his hand and springing back into shape afterward. A few were now beginning to probe and "taste" Grant's body.

"Faster, Cora!"

"But I can't . . ."

"But you can. Hang on to me, will you?"

They shot upward, over the lip of the precipice, to the waiting *Proteus.*

*

Duval helped Michaels up through the hatch.

"What's happening out there?"

Michaels pulled off his helmet, gasping. "Miss Peterson was trapped in the Cells of Hensen. Grant is trying to get her loose but antibodies are swarming over her."

Duval's eyes widened. "What can we do?"

"I don't know. Maybe he can get her back. Otherwise, we've got to go on."

Owens said, "But we can't leave them there."

"Of course not," said Duval, "we've got to go out there, all three of us and . . ." Then, harshly, "Why are you back here, Michaels? Why aren't you out there?"

Michaels looked at Duval hostilely. "Because I wouldn't have done any good. I haven't got Grant's muscles or his reflexes. I'd have been in the way. If you want to help, get out there yourself."

Owens said, "We've got to get them back, alive or . . . or . . . otherwise. They'll be deminiaturizing in about a quarter of an hour."

"All right, then," shouted Duval. "Get into your swim-suit and let's get out there."

"Wait," said Owens. "They're coming. I'll get the hatch ready."

*

Grant's hand was clutching firmly at the wheel of the hatch, while the signal light flashed redly above it. He picked at the antibodies on Cora's back, pinching the wool-like fibers of one between thumb and forefinger, feeling its soft springiness give and then become a wiry core that gave no farther.

He thought: This is a peptide chain.

Dim memories of college courses came back. He had once been able to write the chemical formula of a portion of a peptide chain and here was the real thing. If he had a microscope could he see the individual atoms? No, Michaels had said those would fuzz into nothing no matter what he could do.

He lifted the antibody molecule. It clung tightly at first then gave, sucking free. Neighboring molecules, clinging to it, pulled loose, too. An entire patch came free and Grant swung it away, batting at it. They remained together and came back, seeking their clinging point.

They had no brains, not even the most primitive, and it was wrong to think of them as monsters, or predators, or even fruit flies. They were merely molecules with atoms so arranged as to make them cling to the surfaces that fit theirs through the blind action of inter-atomic forces. A phrase came back to Grant from the recesses of memory: "Van der Waals forces." Nothing more.

He kept pulling at the fuzz on Cora's back. She cried out, "They're coming, Grant. Let's get into the hatch."

Grant looked back. They were finding their way, sensing their presence. Links and chains of them were swooping high above the lip of the precipice and coming down in their general direction like blinded cobras.

Grant said, "We've got to wait . . ." The light turned green. "All right. Now." He whirled at the wheel, desperately.

The antibodies were all about them, but making chiefly for Cora. For her they had already been sensitized and there was far less hesitation now. They clung and joined, spanning her shoulders and making their woolly pattern across her abdomen. They hesitated over the uneven three-dimensional curve of her breasts as though they had not figured that out yet.

Grant had no time to aid Cora in her ineffectual clutchings at the antibodies. He pulled the hatch door open, thrust Cora into it, antibodies and all, and squeezed in after her. The hatch barely held both.

He pushed forcefully against the hatch door while antibodies continued to pour in. The door closed upon their elasticity but the basic wiriness of hundreds of them clogged the door at the end. He bent his back against the pressure of that wiriness and managed to turn the wheel that locked the door in place. A dozen little balls of wool, so soft and almost cuddly when viewed separately and in themselves, wriggled feebly in the crack where the hatch door met the wall. But hundreds of others, untrapped, filled the fluid about them. Air pressure was pushing the fluid out and the hissing filled their ears, but at the moment Grant was concerned only to pull the antibodies loose. Some were settling on his own chest, but that didn't matter. Cora's midriff was buried in them, as was her back. They had formed a solid band about her body from breast to thigh.

She said, "They're tightening, Grant."

Through her mask he could see the agony in her face, and he could hear the effort it took her to speak.

The water was sinking rapidly, but they couldn't wait. Grant hammered at the inner door.

"I . . . I . . . can't brea . . ." gasped Cora.

The door opened, the fluid it still held pouring into the main body of the ship. Duval's hand, thrusting through, seized Cora's arm and pulled her in. Grant followed.

Owens said, "Lord help us, look at them." With an expression of distaste and nausea, he started plucking at the antibodies as Grant had been doing.

A strand tore, then another, then still another. Half-laughing, Grant said, "It's easy, now. Just brush them off."

All were doing so now. They fell into the inch or so of fluid on the floor of the ship and moved feebly.

Duval said, "They're designed to work in body fluid, of

course. Once they're surrounded by air, the molecular attractions alter in nature."

"As long as they're off. Cora . . ."

Cora was breathing in deep, shuddering gasps. Gently, Duval removed her headpiece, but it was to Grant's arm she clung as she suddenly burst into tears.

"I was so *scared,*" she sobbed.

"Both of us were," Grant assured her. "Will you stop thinking it's a disgrace to be frightened? There's a purpose to fear, you know." He was stroking her hair slowly. "It makes the adrenalin flow so that you can swim that much faster and longer and endure that much more. An efficient fear-mechanism is good basic material for heroism."

Duval pushed Grant impatiently to one side, "Are you all right, Miss Peterson?"

Cora took a deep breath and said, with an effort but in a steady voice, "Quite all right, Doctor."

Owens said, "We've got to get out of here." He was in the bubble. "We have practically no time left."

CHAPTER 16 BRAIN

IN THE CONTROL ROOM, the television receivers seemed to spring back into life. "General Carter . . ."

"Yes, what now?"

"They're moving again, sir. They're out of the ear and heading rapidly for the clot."

"Hah! They survived!" He looked at the time-recorder, which read 12. "Twelve minutes." Vaguely, he looked about for the cigar and found it on the floor where he had dropped it and then stepped on it. He picked it up, looked at its flatly mangled shape and threw it away in disgust.

"Twelve minutes. Can they still make it, Reid?"

Reid was crumpled in his chair, looking miserable. "They can make it. They can even get rid of the clot, maybe. But . . ."

"But?"

"But I don't know if we can get them out in time. We can't probe into the brain to pull them out, you know. If we could do that, we would have been able to probe into it for the clot in the first place. That means they've got to get to the brain and then proceed to some point where they *can* be removed. If they don't . . ."

Carter said, querulously. "I've been brought two cups of coffee and one cigar and I haven't had one sip or one puff . . ."

"They're reaching the base of the brain, sir," came the word.

*

Michaels was back at his chart. Grant was at his shoulder, staring at the complexities before him.

"Is that the clot here?"

"Yes," said Michaels.

"It looks a long distance off. We only have twelve minutes."

"It's not as far away as it looks. We'll have clear sailing now. We'll be at the base of the brain in less than a minute and from there, in no time at all . . ."

There was a sudden flood of light pouring in all about the ship. Grant looked up in astonishment and saw, outside, a tremendous wall of milky light, its boundaries invisible.

"The eardrum," said Michaels. "On the other side, the outside world."

An almost unbearably poignant homesickness pulled at Grant. He had almost forgotten that there was an outside world. It seemed to him at the moment that all his life he had been traveling endlessly through a nightmare world of tubes and monsters, a Flying Dutchman of the circulatory system . . . But there it was, the light of the outside world, filtering through the eardrum.

Michaels said, bending over the chart, "You ordered me back into the ship from the hair cells, didn't you, Grant?"

"Yes, I did, Michaels. I wanted you on the ship, not at the hair cells."

"You tell that to Duval. His attitude . . ."

"Why worry? His attitude is always unpleasant, isn't it?"

"This time he was insulting. I don't pretend to be a hero . . ."

"I'll bear witness on your behalf."

"Thank you, Grant. And — and keep an eye on Duval."

Grant laughed. "Of course."

Duval approached, almost as though he realized he was being discussed, and said brusquely, "Where are we, Michaels?"

Michaels looked at him with a bitter expression and said, "We're about to enter the sub-arachnoid cavity. Right at the base of the brain," he added, in Grant's direction.

"All right. Suppose we go in past the oculomotor nerve."

"All right," said Michaels. "If that will give you the most favorable shot at the clot, that's how we'll go in."

Grant backed away, and bent his head to get into the storage room, where Cora was lying on a cot.

She made as though to get up, but he lifted his hand. "Don't. Stay there." And he sat on the floor beside her, knees up and enclosed in his arms. He smiled at her.

She said, "I'm all right now. I'm just malingering, lying here."

"Why not? You're the most beautiful malingerer I've ever seen. Let's malinger together for a minute, if you don't think that sounds too improper."

She smiled in her turn. "It would be difficult for me to complain that you were too forward. After all, you seem to make a career of saving my life."

"All part of a shrewd and extraordinarily subtle campaign to place you under an obligation to me."

"I am! Most decidedly!"

"I'll remind you of that at the proper time."

"Please do. But Grant, really, thank you."

"I like your thanking me, but it's my job. That's why I was sent along. Remember, I make decisions on policy and I take care of emergencies."

"But that's not all, is it?"

"It's quite enough," protested Grant. "I plug snorkels into lungs, pull seaweed out of intakes and most of all I hold on to beautiful women."

"But that's *not* all, is it? You're here to keep an eye on Dr. Duval, aren't you?"

"Why do you say that?"

"Because it's true. The higher echelons at the CMDF don't trust Dr. Duval. They never have."

"Why is that?"

"Because he is a dedicated man, completely innocent and completely involved. He offends others not because he wants to, but because he honestly doesn't know he's offensive. He doesn't know that anything exists beside his work . . ."

"Not even beautiful assistants?"

Cora flushed. "I suppose . . . not even assistants. But he values my work; he really does."

"He'd keep right on valuing your work, wouldn't he, if someone else valued *you?*"

Cora looked away, then went on firmly, "But he's *not* disloyal. One trouble is he favors free exchange of information with the Other Side and says so because he doesn't know *how* to keep his views unobtrusive. Then, when others disagree with him he tells them how foolish he thinks they are."

Grant nodded. "Yes, I can imagine. And that makes everybody love him because people just adore being told how foolish they are."

"Well, that's the way he is."

"Look. Don't sit there and worry. I don't mistrust Duval, any more than I do anyone else."

"Michaels does."

"I know that. Michaels has moments where he mistrusts everyone, both in this ship and outside. He even mistrusts me. But I assure you I give that only the weight I think it deserves."

Cora looked anxious. "You mean Michaels thinks I deliberately damaged the laser? That Dr. Duval and I — together — "

"I think he thinks of that as a possibility."

"And you, Grant?"

"I think of it as a possibility, too."

"But do you believe it?"

"It is a possibility, Cora. Among many possibilities. Some possibilities are better than others. Let me worry about that end of it, dear."

Before she could answer, both heard Duval's voice raised in anger: "No, no, no. It's out of the question, Michaels. I won't have a jackass tell me what to do."

"Jackass! Shall I tell you what you are, you son . . ."

Grant was out front, Cora directly behind him.

Grant said, "Hold it, both of you. What's up?"

Duval turned and said, fuming, "I have the laser back in order. The wire is shaved to the proper size; it's joined to the transistor; and it's back in place. I've just told that to this jackass here . . ." He turned his face toward Michaels and clipped out, "Jackass, I said," then went on, "because he asked me about it."

"Well, good," said Grant. "What's wrong with that?"

Michaels said, heatedly, "Because that son of a bitch saying so doesn't make it so. He's put some things together. I can do that much. Anyone can. How does he know it will *work*?"

"Because I *know*. I've worked with lasers for twelve years. I know when they work."

"Well, then, show us, Doctor. Let us share your knowledge. *Use* it!"

"No! Either it works or it doesn't work. If it doesn't work, I can't fix it under any circumstances because I've done all I can and nothing further can be done. That means we'll be no worse off if I wait till we get to the clot to find out that it doesn't work. But if it works, and it *will* work, it remains jerry-rigged. I don't know how long it will last; a dozen blasts or so at most. I want to save every one of those blasts for the clot. I won't waste a single one of them here. I won't have the mission fail because I tested the laser even once."

"I tell you, you've got to test the laser," said Michaels. "If you don't, then I swear, Duval, that when we get back, I will have you thrown out of the CMDF so far and have you broken into so many small pieces . . ."

"I'll worry about that when we get back. Meanwhile this is my laser and I do as I please with it. You can't order me to do anything I don't wish to do, and neither can Grant."

Grant shook his head. "I'm not ordering you to do anything, Dr. Duval."

Duval nodded briefly and turned away.

Michaels looked after him. "I'll get him."

"He makes sense in this case, Michaels," said Grant. "Are you sure you're not annoyed with him for personal reasons?"

"Because he calls me coward and jackass? Am I supposed to love him for that? But whether I have personal animosity against him or not doesn't matter. I think he's a traitor."

Cora said, angrily, "That's quite untrue."

"I doubt," said Michaels freezingly, "that you're a reliable witness in this case. But never mind. We're getting to the clot and we'll see about Duval then."

"He'll clear that clot," said Cora, "if the laser works."

"If it works," said Michaels. "And if it does, I wouldn't be surprised if he kills Benes — and not by accident."

*

Carter had his jacket off and his sleeves rolled up. He was slumped in his chair on the base of his spine and a second cigar, freshly-lit, was in his mouth. He wasn't puffing.

"In the brain?" he said.

Reid's mustache seemed bedraggled at last. He rubbed his eyes. "Practically at the clot. They've stopped."

Carter looked at the time-recorder, which read 9.

He felt used up, out of juice, out of adrenalin, out of tension, out of life. He said, "Think they'll make it?"

Reid shook his head. "No, I don't."

In nine minutes, maybe ten, the men, ship and all, would be standing full size before them, exploding Benes' body, if they hadn't gotten out in time.

Carter thought of what the newspapers would make of CMDF if this project failed. He heard the speeches from every politican in the land, and from those on the Other Side. How far would CMDF be set back? How many months, years, would it take it to recover?

Wearily, he began to write his letter of resignation in his mind.

*

"We've entered the brain itself," announced Owens, with controlled excitement.

He doused the ship's lights again and all of them looked forward in a moment of wonder that put everything else, even the climax of the mission, out of their minds for a moment.

Duval murmured, "How wonderful. The supreme peak of Creation."

Grant, for the moment, felt that. Surely the human brain was the most intensely complicated object crowded into the smallest possible volume in all the universe.

There was a silence about their surroundings. The cells they could see were jagged, uneven, with fibrous dendrites jutting out here and there, like a bramble bush. As they drifted through the interstitial fluid along passageways between the cells, they could see the dendrites tangling overhead and for a moment they were passing under what seemed the twisted limbs of a row of ancient forest trees.

Duval said, "See, they don't touch. You can see the synapses clearly; always that gap which must be jumped across chemically."

Cora said, "They seem to be full of lights."

Michaels said, an edge of anger still in his voice, "A mere illusion. The reflection of miniaturized light plays tricks. It bears no relation to reality."

"How do you know?" demanded Duval, at once. "This is an important field for study. The reflection of miniaturized light is bound to vary subtly with the structure of the molecular contents of the cell. This sort of reflection, I predict, will become a more powerful instrument for studying the micro-details of the cell than any now existing. It may well be that the techniques arising out of this mission of ours will be far more important than what happens to Benes."

"Is that how you're excusing yourself, Doctor?" asked Michaels.

Duval reddened. "Explain that!"

"Not now," said Grant, imperiously. "Not one more word, gentlemen."

Duval drew a deep breath and turned back to the window.

Cora said, "But anyway, do you see the lights? Watch up above. Watch that dendrite as it comes close."

"I see it," said Grant. The usual glittering reflections did not, as had been generally true elsewhere in the body, sparkle from this point and that randomly, making the whole look like a dense cloud of fireflies. Instead, the sparkle chased itself along the dendrite, a new one beginning before the old one had completed its path.

Owens said, "You know what it looks like? Anyone ever see films of old-fashioned advertising signs with electric lights? With waves of light and dark moving along?"

"Yes," said Cora. "That's *exactly* what it's like. But why?"

Duval said, "A wave of depolarization sweeps along a nerve fiber when it is stimulated. The ion concentrations change;

sodium ion enters the cell. This changes the charge intensity inside and out and lowers the electric potential. Somehow that must affect the reflection of miniaturized light — which is exactly the point I was making — and what we see is the wave of depolarization."

Now that Cora had pointed out the fact, or perhaps because they were moving ever deeper into the brain, the moving wave of sparkles could be seen everywhere; moving along the cells, climbing and descending fibers, twisting into an unimaginably complex system which seemed, at first glance, without any form of order, and yet which gave the sense of order, anyway.

"What we see," said Duval, "is the essence of humanity. The cells are the physical brain, but those moving sparkles represent thought, the human mind."

"Is that the essence?" said Michaels, harshly. "I would have thought it was the soul. Where is the human soul, Duval?"

"Because I can't point it out, do you think it doesn't exist?" demanded Duval. "Where is Benes' genius? You are in his brain. Point to his genius."

"Enough!" said Grant.

Michaels called up to Owens. "We're almost there. Cross over into the capillary at the indicated point. Just push through."

Duval said thoughtfully, "That's the awesome thing of it. We're not just in the mind of a man. This, all about us, is the mind of a scientific genius; someone I would put almost on a par with Newton."

He was silent for a moment and then quoted:

"'*. . . Where the statue stood*
Of Newton with his prism and silent face.
The marble index of a mind . . .'"

Grant cut in, with an awed whisper:

*"'. . . forever
Voyaging through strange seas of thought, alone.'"*

Again a short silence, and Grant said, "Do you think Wordsworth ever thought of this, or could have, when he spoke of 'strange seas of thought.' This is the literal sea of thought, isn't it? And strange it is, too."

Cora said, "I didn't think of you as the poetic type, Grant."

Grant nodded. "All muscle, no mind. That's me."

"Don't be offended."

Michaels said, "When you are done with mumbling poetry, gentlemen, look ahead."

He pointed. They were in the blood stream again, but the red corpuscles (bluish in color) drifted without any definite motion, shuddering slightly in response to Brownian motion, no more. Up ahead was a shadow.

A forest of dendrites could be seen through the transparent walls of the capillary; each strand, each twig with its line of sparkle moving along itself, but more slowly now, and still more slowly. And after a certain point, there were no more sparkles.

The *Proteus* came to a halt. For an instant or two, there was silence, then Owens said quietly, "That's our destination, I think."

Duval nodded. "Yes. The clot."

CHAPTER 17 CLOT

DUVAL SAID, "Notice how the nerve action ends at the clot. That's visible evidence of nerve damage; possibly irreversible. I wouldn't swear that we can help Benes now, even if we remove the clot."

"Good thinking, Doctor," said Michaels, sarcastically. "That excuses you, doesn't it?"

"Shut up, Michaels," said Grant, coldly.

Duval said, "On with the swim suit, Miss Peterson. This has got to be done right now. And put it on inside out. The antibodies are sensitized to its normal surface and there may be some about."

Michaels smiled wearily. "Don't trouble yourselves. It's too late." He pointed to the time-recorder, which was just making the slow, slow change from 7 to 6. He said, "You couldn't possibly perform the operation in time to allow us to get to the removal point in the jugular. Even if you succeed in the removal of the clot, we'll end by deminiaturizing right here and killing Benes."

Duval did not stop in his donning of the suit. Nor did Cora. Duval said, "Well, then, he'll be no worse off than he will be if we don't operate."

"No, but we will. We'll get larger slowly at first. It may take us a whole minute to reach a size that will attract the attention of a white blood cell. There are millions of them around the site of the injury. We'll be engulfed."

"So?"

"I doubt that either the *Proteus* or we could withstand the physical strain placed upon us by the compression within a digestive vacuole inside a white cell. Not in our miniaturized state, and not after all the ship and we have already gone through. We'll continue expanding, but when we are back to full size, it will be as a crushed ship and crushed human beings. You had better leave here, Owens, and make it as quickly as you can for the removal point."

"Hold it," interposed Grant, angrily. "Owens, how long will it take us to removal point?"

Owens said, faintly, "Two minutes!"

"That leaves us four minutes. Maybe more. Isn't it true that deminiaturization after sixty minutes is a conservative estimate? Couldn't we remain miniaturized for longer, if the field holds a little longer than expected."

"Maybe," said Michaels, flatly, "but don't kid yourself. A minute longer. Two minutes at the outside. We can't beat the Uncertainty Principle."

"All right. Two minutes. And mightn't it take longer to deminiaturize than we're counting on?"

Duval said, "It might take a minute or two, if we're lucky."

Owens put in, "It's because of the random nature of the basic structure of the universe. With luck, if everything breaks our way . . ."

"But only a minute or two," said Michaels, "at most."

"All right," said Grant, "we've got four minutes, plus maybe two minutes extra, plus maybe a minute of slow deminiaturization before we do damage to Benes. That's seven minutes of our long, time-distorted variety. Get going, Duval."

"All you'll succeed in doing, you damned fool, is to get Benes killed and us with him," yelled Michaels. "Owens, get us over to removal point."

Owens hesitated.

Grant moved quickly to the ladder and climbed up to Owens' bubble. He said quietly. "Turn off the power, Owens. Turn it off."

Owens' finger moved to a switch, hovered over it. Grant's hand moved quickly to it and flicked it into the OFF position with a strenuous gesture. "Now get down. Come on down."

He half-pulled Owens out of his seat, and both came down. The whole had taken a few seconds and Michaels had watched, open-mouthed, too startled to move.

"What the devil have you done?" he demanded.

"The ship is staying right here," said Grant, "till the operation has succeeded. Now Duval, get on with it."

Duval said, "Get the laser, Miss Peterson." Both were in their swim suits now. Cora's looked sadly seamed and lumpy.

She said, "I must be a rare sight."

Michaels said, "Are you mad? All of you? There is no time. All this is suicide. Listen to me." He was almost frothing with anxiety. "You can't accomplish anything."

Grant said, "Owens, operate the hatch for them."

Michaels flung himself forward, but Grant seized him, whirled him around, and said, "Don't make me hit you, Dr. Michaels. My muscles ache and I don't want to have to use them but if I hit, I will hit hard and, I promise you, I will break your jaw."

Michaels lifted his fists almost as though he were ready to

accept the challenge. But Duval and Cora had disappeared into the hatch and Michaels, watching them leave, became almost pleading.

"Listen, Grant, don't you see what's happening? Duval will kill Benes. It will be so easy. A slip of the laser and who will tell the difference? If you do as I say, we can leave Benes alive, get out and try again tomorrow."

"He may not be alive tomorrow and we can't miniaturize for quite a while, someone said."

"He *might* be alive tomorrow; he'll certainly be dead if you don't stop Duval. Other people can be miniaturized tomorrow, even if we can't."

"In another ship? Nothing but the *Proteus* can manage, or is available."

Michaels became shrill. "Grant, I tell you Duval is an enemy agent."

"I don't believe that," said Grant.

"Why? Because he's so religious? Because he's so full of pious platitudes? Isn't that just the disguise he'd choose? Or have you been influenced by his mistress, his two-bit . . ."

Grant said, "Don't finish that sentence, Michaels! Now, listen. There's no evidence that he's an enemy agent, and there's no reason for me to believe that."

"But I'm *telling* you . . ."

"I know you are. The fact is, though, I happen to believe that *you* are the enemy agent, Dr. Michaels."

"*I?*"

"Yes. I have no real evidence for that either; nothing that could hold up in a law court, but once security is through with you, such evidence will be found, I think."

Michaels pushed away from Grant and stared at him with horror. "Of course, I see now. *You* are the agent, Grant. Owens, don't you see? There were a dozen times when we could have gotten out safely, when it was obvious that the mission couldn't succeed, and wouldn't. He kept us in here every time. That's why he worked so hard replenishing our air supply at the lung. That's why . . . help me, Owens. Help me."

Owens stood irresolute.

Grant said, "The time-recorder is about to move to five. We now have three minutes more. Give me three minutes, Owens. You know that Benes won't live unless we remove the clot in those three minutes. I'll go out and help them and you keep Michaels immobilized. If I'm not back by the reading of two, get out of here and save the ship and yourself. Benes will die and maybe we will, too. But you'll be safe and you can put the finger on Michaels."

Owens still said nothing.

Grant said, "Three minutes." And he began putting on his suit. The time-recorder said 5.

Owens said, finally, "Three minutes, then. All right. But only three minutes."

Michaels sat down wearily. "You're letting them kill Benes, Owens, but I've done what I could. My conscience is clear."

Grant worked his way through the hatch.

*

Duval and Cora swam quickly in the direction of the clot, he carrying the laser, she the power unit.

Cora said, "I don't see any white cells, do you?"

"I'm not looking for them," said Duval, brusquely.

He looked thoughtfully ahead. The beam of the ship's headlight and their own smaller ones were weakened by the tangle of fibers that seemed to encase the clot just on the other side of the point at which the nerve impulses appeared to stop. The wall of the arteriole had been abraded by the injury and was not entirely blocked by the clot, which embraced the section of nerve fibers and cells tightly.

"If we can break up the clot and relieve the pressure without touching the nerve itself," muttered Duval, "we will be doing well. If we leave only a basic scab to keep the arteriole plugged. Let's see now."

He maneuvered for position and raised the laser. "And if this thing works."

Cora said, "Dr. Duval, remember you said that the most economical stroke would be from above."

"I remember exactly," said Duval, grimly, "and I intend to hit it precisely."

He pressed the laser trigger. For the barest moment, a thin beam of coherent light flashed into being.

"It works," cried Cora, gladly.

"This time," said Duval. "But it will have to work a number of times."

For a moment, the clot had stood out in relief against the unbearable brilliance of the laser beam and a line of small bubbles formed and marked out its path. Now the darkness was greater than before.

Duval said, "Close one eye, Miss Peterson, so that its retina will not require resensitization."

Again the laser beam, and when it was over Cora closed her open eye and opened the closed one. She said, excitedly, "It's working, Dr. Duval. The glitter is progressing out of sight now. A whole dark area is lighting up."

Grant was swimming up to them. "How's it coming, Duval?"

"Not bad," said Duval. "If I can cut it through transversely now and relieve the pressure on one key spot, I think the entire nerve pathway will be freed."

He swam to one side.

Grant called after him, "We have less than three minutes."

"Don't bother me," said Duval.

Cora said, "It's all right, Grant. He'll do it. Did Michaels make trouble?"

"Some," said Grant, grimly. "Owens has him under guard."

"Under guard?"

"Just in case . . ."

*

Inside the *Proteus,* Owens cast quick glances outward. "I'll be damned if I know what to do," he muttered.

"Just stand here and let the murderers work," said Michaels, sarcastically. "You'll be held responsible for this, Owens."

Owens was silent.

Michaels said, "You can't believe I'm an enemy agent."

Owens said, "I'm not believing anything. Let's wait for the two minute mark and if they're not back, we'll leave. What's wrong with that?"

"All right," said Michaels.

Owens said, "The laser is working. I saw the flash. And you know . . ."

"What?"

"The clot. I can see the sparkle of the nerve action in that direction where it couldn't be seen before."

"I don't," said Michaels, peering outward.

"I do," said Owens. "I tell you, it's working. And they'll be back. It looks as though you were wrong, Michaels."

Michaels shrugged. "All right, so much the better. If I'm wrong and if Benes lives, I could ask for nothing more. Only," his voice grew tightly alarmed. "Owens!"

"What?"

"There's something wrong with the escape hatch. That damned fool Grant must have been too excited to close it properly. Or was it excitement?"

"But what's wrong? I don't see anything."

"Are you blind? It's seeping fluid. Look at the seam."

"It's been wet here since Cora and Grant got away from the antibodies. Don't you remember . . ."

Owens was staring down at the hatch and Michaels' hand,

having closed around the screwdriver Grant had used to open the wireless panel, brought its handle down hard upon Owens' head.

With a muffled exclamation, Owens dropped to his knees, dazed.

Michaels struck again in a fever of impatience and began jamming the limp figure into its swim suit. Perspiration stood out on his bald head in great drops. Opening the escape hatch, he thrust Owens into it. Quickly, he let the hatch fill with water, then opened the outer door by the panel control, losing a precious moment searching for it.

Ideally, he should now have flipped the ship to make certain that Owens had been thrown clear, but there was no time.

No time, he thought, no time.

Frantically, he leaped to the bubble and studied the controls. Something would have to be thrown to start the engine. Ah, there! A thrill of triumph surged through him as he felt the distant drumming of the engines begin again.

He looked ahead toward the clot. Owens had been right. A glitter of light was racing down the length of a long nerve process which until then had been dark.

*

Duval was aiming the laser beam in short bursts at quick intervals.

Grant said, "I think we've just about had it, Doctor. Time's gone."

"I'm just about done. The clot has crumbled away. Just one portion. Ah . . . Mr. Grant, the operation has been a success."

"And we've got maybe three minutes to get out, maybe two. Back to the ship, now . . ."

Cora said, "Someone else is here."

Grant veered, lunged toward the aimlessly swimming figure. "Michaels!" he cried. Then, "No, it's Owens. What . . ."

Owens said, "I don't know. He hit me, I think. I don't know how I got out here."

"Where's Michaels?"

"On the ship, I sup . . ."

Duval cried, "The ship's motors have started!"

"What!" said Owens, startled. "Who . . ."

"Michaels," said Grant. "Obviously he must be at the controls."

"Why did you leave the ship, Grant?" demanded Duval, angrily.

"It's what I'm asking myself now. I had hoped Owens . . ."

"I'm sorry," said Owens, "I didn't think he was really an enemy agent. I couldn't tell . . ."

Grant said, "The trouble is I wasn't completely certain of it myself. Now, of course . . ."

"An enemy agent!" said Cora, with horror.

Michaels' voice sounded. "All of you, back off. In two minutes, the white cells will have come and by that time, I'll be on the way out. I'm sorry, but you had your chance to come out with me."

The ship was angling high now, and making a large curve.

"He's got it under full acceleration," said Owens.

"And," said Grant, "I think he's aiming at the nerve."

"Exactly what I'm doing, Grant," came Michaels' voice, grimly. "Rather dramatic, don't you think? First, I'll ruin the work of that mouthing saint, Duval, not so much for the sake of that alone as to do the kind of damage that will call a cohort of white cells to the scene at once. They'll take care of you."

Duval shouted, "Listen! Think! Why do this? Think of your country!"

"I'm thinking of mankind," shouted back Michaels, furiously. "The important thing is to keep the military out of the picture. Unlimited deminiaturization in their hands will destroy the earth. If you fools can't see that . . ."

The *Proteus* was now diving directly for the just-relieved nerve process.

Grant said desperately, "The laser! Let me have the laser!"

He snatched the instrument from Duval, forcing it away. Where's the trigger? Never mind. I've got it."

He angled upward, trying to intercept the hurtling ship. "Give me maximum power," he called to Cora. "Full power!"

He took careful aim and a pencil-wide beam of light emerged from the laser, and flickered out.

Cora said, "The laser gave out, Grant."

"Here, then, you hold it. I think I got the *Proteus*, though."

It was hard to tell. In the general dimness there was no way to see clearly.

"You struck the rudder, I think," said Owens. "You've killed my ship." Behind his mask, his cheeks were suddenly wet.

"Whatever you struck," said Duval, "the ship doesn't seem to be handling very well."

The *Proteus* was shaking now indeed, its headlight flashing up and down in a wide arc. The ship pulled downward, crashed through the arteriole wall, missed the nerve by a hand's breath and lunged down into a forest of dendrites; catching and breaking free and catching again, until it lay there, a bubble of metal, entangled in thick, smooth fibers.

"He missed the nerve," said Cora.

"He did damage enough," growled Duval. "That may start a new clot — or maybe not. I hope not. In any case the white cells will be here. We had better leave."

"Where?" said Owens.

"If we follow the optic nerve, we can make it to the eye in a minute or less. Follow me."

"We can't leave the ship," said Grant. "It will deminiaturize."

"Well, we can't take it with us," said Duval. "We have no choice but to try to save our own lives."

"We can still do something, perhaps," insisted Grant. "How much time do we have left?"

Duval said emphatically, "None! I think we're beginning to deminiaturize now. In a minute or so we'll be large enough to attract the attention of a white cell."

"Deminiaturizing? Now? I don't feel it."

"You won't. But the surroundings are slightly smaller than they've been. Let's go."

Duval took a quick view around for orientation. "Follow me," he said again, and began swimming away.

Cora and Owens followed and, after a last moment of hesitation, Grant followed them.

He had failed. In the last analysis, he had failed because, feeling not entirely convinced that Michaels was an enemy on the basis of some uncertain reasoning, he had vacillated.

He would turn himself in, he thought bitterly, as a jackass unfit for his job.

•

"But they're not moving," said Carter, savagely. "They stay there at the clot. Why? Why? Why?" The time-recorder read 1.

"It's too late for them to get out now," said Reid.

A message came through from the electroencephalographic unit. "Sir, EEG data indicates Benes' brain action is being restored to normal."

Carter yelled, "Then the operation is a success. Why are they staying behind?"

"We have no way of knowing."

The time-recorder moved to 0 and a loud alarm went off. Its shrill jangle filled the entire room with the clang of doom.

Reid raised his voice to be heard. "We've got to take them out."

"It will kill Benes."

"If we don't take them out, *that* will kill Benes, too."

Carter said, "If there's anyone outside the ship, we won't be able to get him out."

Reid shrugged, "We can't help that. The white cells may get them or they may deminiaturize unharmed."

"But Benes will die."

Reid leaned toward Carter, and shouted, "There's nothing to be done about that. *Nothing!* Benes is dead! Do you want to take a chance on killing five more uselessly."

Carter seemed to shrink within himself. He said, "Give the order!"

Reid went to the transmitter. "Remove the *Proteus*," he said quietly, then went on to the window overlooking the operating room.

*

Michaels was only semi-conscious at best when the *Proteus* came to rest in the dendrites. The sudden veering that had come after the bright flash of the laser—it must have been the laser—had thrown him against the panel with great force. The only sensation he had from his right arm now was one of frightful pain. It had to be broken. A section of the wall had been fused, and the gap was closed off only by the surface tension of the plasma.

The air he had left would last him for the minute or two that would remain before deminiaturization. Already, even as he watched, it seemed to his dizzying senses that the dendrite cables had narrowed a bit. They couldn't really be shrinking, so he had to be expanding, very slowly just at first.

At full size, his arm could be taken care of. The others would be killed by white cells and be done with. He would say . . . he would say . . . something that would explain the broken ship. And in any case, Benes would be dead and indefinite miniaturization would die with him. There would be peace . . . peace . . .

He watched the dendrites while his body remained limply draped over the control panel. Could he move? Was he paralyzed? Was his back broken as well as his arm?

Dully, he considered the possibility. He felt his sense of comprehension and awareness slipping away as the dendrites became clouded over with a milky haze.

Milky haze?

A white cell!

Of course, it was a white cell. The ship was larger than the individuals out in the plasma, and it was the ship that was at the site of damage. The ship would be the first to attract the attention of the white cell.

The window of the *Proteus* was coated with sparkling milk. Milk invaded the plasma at the break in the ship's hull in the rear and struggled to break through the surface tension barrier.

The next to the last sound Michaels heard was the hull of the *Proteus,* fragile in its make-up of miniaturized atoms, strained to the breaking point with what it had already been through, cracking and splintering under the assault of the white cell.

The last sound he heard was his own laughter.

CHAPTER 18 EYE

CORA SAW the white cell at almost the time Michaels did.

"Look," she cried in horror.

They stopped, turned to look back.

The white cell was tremendous. It was five times as large in diameter as the *Proteus*, perhaps larger. Compared to the individuals watching, it was a mountain, a mountain of milky, skinless, pulsing protoplasm. Its large, lobed nucleus, a milky shadow within its substance, seemed to be a malevolent, irregular eye, and the shape of the whole creature altered and changed with every moment. A portion bulged toward the *Proteus*.

Grant started toward the *Proteus*, almost as though by reflex action.

Cora seized his arm. "What are you going to do, Grant?"

Duval said, excitedly, "There's no way to save him. You'll be throwing away your life."

Grant shook his head violently. "It's not he I'm thinking of. It's the ship."

Owens said, sadly, "You can't save the ship, either."

"But we might be able to get it out, where it can expand safely. Listen, even if it is crushed by the white cell, even if it is separated into atoms, each miniaturized atom will deminiaturize; it is deminiaturizing right now. It doesn't matter whether Benes is killed by an intact ship or by a pile of splinters."

Cora said, "You can't get the ship out. Oh, Grant, don't die. Not after all this. Please."

Grant smiled at her. "Believe me, I have every reason not to die, Cora. You three keep on going. Let me make just one college try."

He swam back, heart beating in almost unbearable revulsion at the monster he was approaching. There were others behind it, farther off, but he wanted this one; the one that was engulfing the *Proteus,* only this one.

At closer quarters, he could see its surface. A portion in profile showed clear, but within were granules and vacuoles. An intricate mechanism, too intricate for biologists to understand in detail even yet, and all crammed into a single microscopic blob of living matter. The *Proteus* was entirely within it now, a splintering, dark shadow encased in a vacuole. Grant had thought that for a moment he had seen Michaels' face in the bubble, but that might have been only imagination.

Grant was at the heaving, mountainous surface now, but how was he to attract the attention of such a thing? It had neither eyes nor sense, neither a mind nor purpose. It was an automatic machine of protoplasm, designed to respond in certain fashion to injury. How? Grant didn't know. Yet a white cell could tell when a bacterium was in its vicinity. In some cellular way, it knew. It had known when the *Proteus* was near it and it had reacted by engulfing it.

Grant was far smaller than the *Proteus,* far smaller than a bacterium, even now. Was he large enough to be noticed? He had his knife out and sank it deeply into the material before him, slitting it downward. Nothing happened. No gush of blood, for there is no blood in a white cell. Then, slowly, a bulging of the inner protoplasm appeared at the site of the ruptured membrane and that portion of the membrane drew away.

Grant struck again. He didn't want to kill it; he didn't think he could at his present size. But was there some way of attracting its attention?

He drifted off and, with mounting excitement, noticed a bulge in the wall, a bulge pointing toward him. He drifted further away and the bulge followed. He had been noticed. The manner of the noticing he could not say, but the white cell, with everything it contained, with the *Proteus*, was following.

He moved away faster now. The white cell followed but (Grant hoped fervently) not quickly. Grant had reasoned that it was not designed for speed, that it moved like an ameba, bulging out a portion of its substance and then pouring itself into the bulge. Under ordinary conditions it fought with immobile objects, with bacteria or with foreign, inanimate detritus. Its ameboid motion was fast enough for that. Now it would have to deal with an object capable of darting away. (Darting away quickly enough, Grant hoped.) With gathering speed, he swam toward the others, who were still delaying, still watching for him.

He gasped, "Get a move on. I think it's following."

"So are others," said Duval, grimly.

Grant looked about. The distance was swarming with white cells. What one had noticed, all had noticed.

"How . . ."

Duval said, "I saw you strike at the white cell. If you damaged it, chemicals were released into the blood stream, chemicals that attracted white cells from all the neighboring regions."

"Then, for God's sake, *swim!*"

*

The surgical team was gathered around Benes' head, while Carter and Reid watched from above. Carter's mood of black depression was deepening by the moment.

It was over. All for nothing. All for nothing. All for . . .

"General Carter! Sir!" The sound was urgent, strident. The man's voice was cracking with excitement.

"Yes?"

"The *Proteus,* sir. It's moving."

Carter yelled. "Stop surgery!"

Each member of the surgical team looked up in startled wonder.

Reid plucked at Carter's sleeve. "The motion may be the mere effect of the ship's slowly accelerating deminiaturization. If you don't get them now, they will be in danger of the white cells."

"What kind of motion?" shouted Carter. "Where's it heading?"

"Along the optic nerve, sir."

Carter turned fiercely on Reid. "Where does that go? What does it mean?"

Reid's face lit up, "It means an emergency exit I hadn't thought of. They're heading for the eye and out through the lachrymal duct. They may make it. They might just get away with it, damaging one eye at most. Get a microscope slide, someone. Carter, let's get down there."

*

The optic nerve was a bundle of fibers, each like a string of sausages.

Duval paused to place his hand on the junction between two of the "sausages."

"A node of Ranvier," he said, wonderingly, "I'm touching it."

"Don't keep on touching it," gasped Grant. "Keep on swimming."

The white cells had to negotiate the close-packed network and did it less easily than the swimmers could. They had squeezed out into the interstitial fluid and were bulging through the spaces between the nerve fibers.

Grant watched anxiously to make sure that *the* white cell was still in pursuit. The one with the *Proteus* in it. He could not make out the *Proteus* any longer. If it existed in the white cell nearest, it had been transferred so deep into its substance that it was no longer visible. If the white cell behind was not *the* white cell, then Benes might be killed despite everything.

The nerves sparked wherever the beam from the helmet lights struck and the sparkles moved backward in rapid progression.

"Light impulses," muttered Duval. "Benes' eyes aren't entirely closed."

Owens said, "Everything's definitely getting smaller. Do you notice that?"

Grant nodded. "I sure do." The white cell was only half the monster it had been only moments before, if that.

"We only have seconds to go," said Duval.

Cora said, "I can't keep up."

Grant veered toward her. "Sure you can. We're in the eye now. We're only the width of a tear-drop from safety." He put his arm around her waist, pushing her forward, then took the laser and power unit from her.

Duval said, "Through here and we'll be in the lacrymal duct."

They were large enough almost to fill the interstitial space through which they were swimming. As they grew, their speed had increased and the white cells grew less fearsome.

Duval kicked open the membranous wall he had come up against. "Get through," he said, "Miss Peterson, you first."

Grant pushed her through, and followed her. Then Owens and finally Duval.

"We're out," said Duval with a controlled excitement. "We're out of the body."

"Wait," said Grant. "I want that white cell out, too. Otherwise . . ."

He waited a moment, then let out a shout of excitement. "There it is. And, by heaven, it's the right one."

The white cell oozed through the opening that Duval's boot had made, but with difficulty. The *Proteus,* or the shattered splinters of it, could be seen clearly through its substance. It had expanded until it was nearly half the size of the white cell and the poor monster was finding itself with an unexpected attack of indigestion. It struggled on gamely, however. Once it had been stimulated to follow, it could do nothing else.

The three men and a woman drifted upward in a well of rising fluid. The white cell, barely moving, drifted up with them. The smooth, curved wall at one side was transparent. It was transparent not in the fashion of the thin capillary wall, but truly transparent. There were no signs of cell membranes or of nuclei.

Duval said, "This is the cornea. The other wall is the lower eyelid. We've got to get far enough away to deminiaturize fully without hurting Benes, and we only have seconds to do it in."

Up above, many feet above (on their still tiny scale), was a horizontal crack.

"Through there," said Duval.

*

"The ship's on the surface of the eye," came the triumphant shout.

"All right," said Reid. "Right eye."

A technician leaned closer with the microscope slide at Benes' closed eye. A magnifying lens was in place. Slowly, with a felted clamp, the lower eyelid was gently pinched and pulled down.

"It's there," said the technician in hushed tones. "Like a speck of dirt."

Skillfully, he placed the slide to the eye, and a tear-drop with the speck in it squeezed on to it.

Everyone backed away.

Reid said, "Something that is large enough to see is going to get much larger very quickly. Scatter!"

The technician, torn between hurry and the necessity for gentleness, placed the slide down on the floor of the room, then backed away at a quick trot.

The nurses wheeled the operating table quickly through the large double door and with a startlingly accelerated speed, the specks on the slide grew to full size.

Three men, a woman, and a heap of metal fragments, rounded and eroded, were there, where none had been a moment before.

Reid muttered, "Eight seconds to spare."

But Carter said, "Where's Michaels? If Michaels is still in Benes . . ." He started after the vanished operating table with the consciousness of defeat once again filling him.

Grant pulled off his helmet and waved him back. "It's all right, General. That's what's left of the *Proteus* and somewhere in it you'll find whatever's left of Michaels. Maybe just an organic jelly with some fragments of bones."

*

Grant still hadn't grown used to the world as it was. He had slept, with a few breaks, for fifteen hours, and he woke in wonder at a world of light and space.

He had breakfast in bed, with Carter and Reid at his bedside, smiling.

Grant said, "Are the rest getting this treatment, too?"

Carter said, "Everything that money can buy — for a while, anyway. Owens is the only one we've let go. He wanted to be with his wife and kids and we turned him loose, but only after he gave us a quick description of what happened. Apparently, Grant, the mission's success was more to your credit than to anyone's."

"If you want to go by a few items, maybe," said Grant. "If you want to recommend me for a medal and a promotion, I'll accept. If you want to recommend me for a year's vacation with pay, I'll accept them even more quickly. Actually, though, the mission would have been a failure without any one of us. Even Michaels guided us efficiently enough, for the most part."

"Michaels," said Carter, thoughtfully. "That bit about him, you know, isn't for publication. The official story is that he died in the line of duty. It wouldn't do any good to have it known that a traitor had infiltrated the CMDF. And I don't know that he *was* a traitor at that."

Reid said, "I knew him well enough to be able to say that he wasn't. Not in the usual sense of the word."

Grant nodded. "I agree. He wasn't a story-book villain. He took time to put a swim suit on Owens before pushing him out of the ship. He was content to have the white cells kill him, but he couldn't do the job himself. No — I think he really wanted to keep indefinite miniaturization a secret for, as he saw it, the good of humanity."

Reid said, "He was all for peaceful uses of miniaturization. So am I. But what good would it do to . . ."

Carter interrupted. "You're dealing with a mind that grew irrational under pressure. Look, we've had this sort of thing since the invention of the atomic bomb. There are always people who think that if some new discovery with frightful implications is suppressed, all will be well. Except that you *can't* suppress a discovery whose time has come. If Benes had died, indefinite miniaturization would still have been discovered next year, or five years from now, or ten. Only then, They might have had it first."

"And now We will have it first," said Grant, "and what do We do with it? End in the final war? Maybe Michaels was right."

Carter said, dryly, "And maybe the common sense of humanity will prevail on both sides. It has so far."

Reid said, "Especially since, once this story gets out, and the news media spread the tale of the fantastic voyage of the *Proteus,* the peaceful uses of miniaturization will be dramatized to the point where we can all fight military domination of the Technique. And perhaps successfully."

Carter, taking out a cigar, looked grim and did not answer directly. He said, "Tell me, Grant, how did you catch on to Michaels?"

"I didn't really," said Grant. "It was all the result of a confused mass of thinking. In the first place, general, you put me on board ship because you suspected Duval."

"Oh, now . . . wait . . ."

"Everyone on the ship knew you had done so. Except Duval, perhaps. That gave me a headstart — in the wrong direction. However, you were clearly not sure of your ground, for you didn't warn me of anything, so I wasn't inclined to go off half-cocked myself. Those were high-powered people on board ship and I knew if I grabbed someone and turned out to be mistaken, you would back off and let me take the rap."

Reid smiled gently, and Carter flushed and grew very interested in his cigar.

Grant said, "No hard feelings, of course. It's part of my job to take the rap — but only if I have to. So I waited until I was sure, and I was never really sure.

"We were plagued with a series of accidents, or what might possibly have been accidents. For instance, the laser was damaged and there was the chance that Miss Peterson had damaged it. But why in so clumsy a fashion? She knew a dozen ways of gimmicking the laser so that it would seem perfectly all right and yet not work properly. She could have arranged it so that Duval's aim would be off just enough to make it inevitable that he kill the nerve, or perhaps even Benes. A crudely damaged laser was either an accident, then, or the deliberate work of someone other than Miss Peterson.

"Then, too, my lifeline came loose in the lungs and I nearly died as a result. Duval was the logical suspect there, but it was he who suggested that the ship's headlight be shone into the gap, and that saved me. Why try to kill me and then act to save me? It doesn't make sense. Either that was an accident, too, or my lifeline had been loosened by someone other than Duval.

"We lost our air-supply, and Owens might have arranged that little disaster. But then when we pulled in more air, Owens improvised an air-miniaturization device that seemed to do miracles. He could easily not have done so and no one of us would have been able to accuse him of sabotage. Why bother to lose our air and then work like the devil to gain it back? Either that was an accident, too, or the air supply had been sabotaged by someone other than Owens.

"I could omit myself from consideration, since I knew that I wasn't engaged in sabotage. That left Michaels."

Carter said, "You reasoned that he had been responsible for all those accidents."

"No, they might still have been accidents. We'll never know. But if it *were* sabotage then Michaels was far and away the most likely candidate, for he was the only one who was not involved in a last-minute rescue, or who might be expected to have performed a more subtle piece of sabotage. So now let's consider Michaels.

"The first accident was the encounter with the arterio-venous fistula. Either that was an honest misfortune or Michaels had guided us into it deliberately. If this was sabotage, then, unlike all the other cases, only one culprit was conceivable, only one — Michaels. I said as much to Michaels himself at one point. Only he could possibly have guided us into it; only he could possibly know Benes' circulatory system well enough to spot a microscopic fistula; and it was he who directed the exact spot of insertion into the artery in the first place."

Reid said, "It might still have been a misfortune; an honest error."

"True! But whereas in all the other accidents, those who were involved as possible suspects did their best to pull us through, Michaels, after we had emerged into the venous system, argued hard for immediate abandonment of the mission. He did the same at every other crisis. He was the only one to do so consistently. And yet that wasn't the real giveaway as far as I was concerned."

"Well, then, what was the giveaway?" asked Carter.

"When the mission first started and we were miniaturized and inserted into the carotid artery, I was scared. We were all a little uneasy, to say the least, but Michaels was the most frightened of all. He was almost paralyzed with fear. I accepted that at the time. I saw no disgrace in it. As I said, I was pretty frightened myself, and in fact, I was glad of the company. *But . . .*"

"But?"

"But after we had gotten through the arterio-venous fistula, Michaels never showed any trace of fear again. At times when the rest of us were nervous, he was not. He had become a rock. In fact, at the start, he had given me plenty of statements on what a coward he was — to explain his obvious fear — but toward the end of the voyage, he was offended almost to frenzy when Duval implied he was a coward. That change in attitude got to seeming queerer and queerer to me.

"It seemed to me there had to be a special reason for his initial fear. As long as he faced dangers with the rest of us, he was a brave man. Perhaps, then, it was when he faced a danger the rest of us did not share that he was afraid. The inability to share the risk, the necessity to face death alone, was what turned him coward.

"At the start, after all, the rest of us were frightened of the mere act of being miniaturized, but that was carried through safely. After that, we all expected to move toward the clot, operate on it and get out, taking ten minutes, perhaps, all told.

"But Michaels must have been the only one of us who knew this was not going to happen. He alone must have known there would be trouble and that we were about to rumble into a whirlpool. Owens had spoken about the ship's fragility at the briefing and Michaels must have expected death. He alone must have expected death. No wonder he nearly broke down.

"When we got through the fistula in one piece, he was almost delirious with relief. After that, he felt certain that we would not be able to complete the mission and he relaxed. With each successful surmounting of some crisis, he grew angrier. He had no more room for fear, only for anger.

"By the time we were in the ear, I had made up my mind that Michaels, not Duval, was our man. I wouldn't let him badger Duval into trying the laser beforehand. I ordered him away from Miss Peterson when I was trying to get her away from the antibodies. But then, in the end, I made a mistake. I didn't stay with him during the actual operation and that gave him his chance to seize the ship. There was this last little shred of doubt in my mind . . ."

"That perhaps it was Duval after all?" said Carter.

"I'm afraid so. So I went out to watch the operation when I could have done nothing about it even if Duval *were* a traitor. If it hadn't been for that final piece of stupidity, I might have brought the ship back intact, and Michaels alive."

"Well," Carter got to his feet, "it was cheap at the price. Benes is alive and slowly recovering. I'm not sure that Owens thinks so, though. He's in mourning for his ship."

"I don't blame him," said Grant, "it was a sweet vessel. Uh — listen, where's Miss Peterson, do you know?"

Reid said, "Up and around. She had more stamina than you had, apparently."

"I mean, is she here at the CMDF anywhere?"

"Yes. In Duval's office, I imagine."

"Oh," said Grant, suddenly deflated. "Well, I'll wash and shave and get out of here."

*

Cora put the papers together. "Well, then, Dr. Duval, if the report can wait over the weekend, I would appreciate the time off."

"Yes, certainly," said Duval. "I think we could all use some time off. How do you feel?"

"I seem to be all right."

"It's been an experience, hasn't it?"

Cora smiled and walked toward the door.

The corner of Grant's head pushed past it. "Miss Peterson?"

Cora started violently, recognized Grant, and came running to him, smiling. "It was Cora in the blood stream."

"Is it still Cora?"

"Of course. It always will be, I hope."

Grant hesitated. "You might call me Charles. You might even get to the point someday where you can call me Good Old Charlie."

"I'll try, Charles."

"When do you quit work?"

"I've just quit for the weekend."

Grant thought a while, rubbed his clean-shaven chin, then nodded toward Duval, who was bent over his desk.

"Are you all tied up with him?" he asked at last.

Cora said, gravely, "I admire his work. He admires my work." And she shrugged.

Grant said, "May I admire *you?*"

She hesitated, then smiled a little. "Any time you want to. As long as you want to. If . . . if I can admire you occasionally, too."

"Let me know when and I'll strike a pose."

They laughed together. Duval looked up, saw them in the doorway, smiled faintly, and waved something that might have been either a greeting or a farewell.

Cora said, "I want to change into street clothes, and then I would like to see Benes. Is that all right?"

"Will they allow visitors?"

Cora shook her head. "No. But we're special."

*

Benes' eyes were open. He tried to smile.

A nurse whispered anxiously, "Only a minute, now. He doesn't know what's happened, so don't say anything about it."

"I understand," said Grant.

To Benes, in a low voice, he said, "How are you?"

Benes tried again to smile. "I'm not sure. Very tired. I have a headache and my right eye hurts, but I seem to have survived."

"Good!"

"It takes more than a knock on the head to kill a scientist," said Benes. "All that mathematics makes the skull as hard as a rock, eh?"

"We're all glad of that," said Cora, gently.

"Now I must remember what I came here to tell. It's a little hazy, but it's coming back. It's all in me, all of it." And now he did smile.

And Grant said, "You'd be surprised at what's in you, Professor."

The nurse ushered them out and Grant and Cora left, hand in warm hand, into a world that suddenly seemed to hold no terrors for them, but only the prospect of great joy.